DEVASTATOR

The Black Coat Script Library

1. Randy & Jean-Marc Lofficier – *Despair* (based on a novel by Marc Agapit; illustrations by Sylvain Despretz)
2. Mike Baron – *The Iron Triangle*
3. Emma Bull & Will Shetterly – *War for the Oaks* (based on a novel by Emma Bull)
4. Steve Englehart – *Majorca*
5. Emma Bull & Will Shetterly – *Nightspeeder* (illustrations by Kevin O'Neill)
6. Andrew Paquette – *Peripheral Vision*
7. James D. Hudnall – *Devastator* (based on his comic book)

forthcoming

8. Marv Wolfman – *Unexplained*
9. Roy Thomas & Gerry Conway – *Doc Dynamo*

DEVASTATOR

screenplay by
James D. Hudnall

based on his comic book

A Black Coat Press Book

Acknowledgements: Thanks to Greg Horn, David Engel, Neal Tabachnick and to David McDonnell for proofreading the typescript.

Visit our website at www.blackcoatpress.com

ISBN 1-932983-20-1. First Printing. October 2004. Published by Black Coat Press, an imprint of Hollywood Comics.com, LLC, P.O. Box 17270, Encino, CA 91416. All rights reserved. Except for review purposes, no part of this book may be reproduced or transmitted in any form or by any means, electronic or mechanical, including photocopying, recording or by any information storage and retrieval system, without permission in writing from the publisher. The stories and characters depicted in this book are entirely fictional. Printed in the United States of America.

Introduction

Devastator is my first screenplay and it's been a long time coming. In the late '80s, I started talking to a couple producers down in L.A. who had read my *Lex Luthor: The Unauthorized Biography*. They asked me if I had any screenplays they could read and I said no, but I could come up with something. So I sat down and put together a 15-page outline that is the story you hold in your hands. It combined my love of martial arts and science fiction. I was especially into cyberpunk stories at the time, so I thought a cyberpunk martial arts movie would be really cool. No one had thought of that before. (This was at least ten years before *The Matrix*.)

Well, they liked the story OK, but I'm not sure they were into it. I started on the screenplay but sort of crapped out about half-way in. Years passed and I got it finished, but it wasn't quite up to snuff. I had made a lot of mistakes that many first time screenwriters do. It needed more drafts.

By then, I had moved to L.A. and met a guy named David Engel who was working his way up through the system. Dave wanted to be a producer. He knew a friend of mine, so we all hung out together. Dave wanted to help me get my comics made into film and television. We became friends and, eventually, *Devastator* came up. Dave suggested I finish it so I could have a sample.

I did new drafts; Dave gave me copious notes, which were mostly to whip it into shape so that it was saleable. He had been a script reader for years so he knew what they were looking for. So, for a couple months, I worked and worked on it, until we had something we thought was good enough.

But I felt it still wasn't quite there. I just couldn't figure out why.

I got busy with things, Dave got busy with stuff of his own. We showed the screenplay around, got some interest, but no bites.

Since I hate to let anything go to waste, I decided to convert it to a comic. So I talked to my friend, artist Greg Horn, who was doing *ESPers* with me at the time, and asked him if he was interested in doing *Devastator*. We managed to get two issues out through Image, but sales didn't warrant the third. Once again, I felt there was something I should do to improve it.

Meanwhile, we showed it to people. Had a director really interested in it at one point and wanted to make a TV show or movie out of it, but he ended up doing some other comics-related project. And still I wanted to keep it alive.

So when Black Coat Press asked me if I had a screenplay they could publish, I selected *Devastator* (out of the five I've done to date) because it was my first and I still think it rocks. I just wanted to spruce it up.

This draft changes the nature of the e-drugs, which originally were computer chips you plugged into a socket in the back of your neck. I thought, you know, that's kind of creepy, even though people get their faces pierced and so on, these days. It's still probably off-putting to some people. So I figured the chip could be in a patch that makes its connection through an implant that's under the skin.

I also brushed up the dialogue and updated some of the tech. When I wrote this story, flat screen TVs and hand-held computers were science fiction. Now, they're commonplace. I modified some descriptions so they were more in line with what people understand today. I also tightened up a lot of the dialogue which was kind of wordy. (I'm always looking for things to improve.)

Anyway, here you go. The latest draft of *Devastator*.

Hope you like it. It was a lot of hard work, but I'm much happier with it now.

James D. Hudnall

DEVASTATOR

Devastator

FADE IN:

<u>EXT. CITYSCAPE - NIGHT</u>
GRAPHIC: LOS ANGELES - 2019

Skyscrapers dominate the city like obnoxious giants. Video billboards plaster the sides, running commercials non-stop. The entire surface of some buildings are towering video screens, making the city seem alive with sight and color.

It's as if the city has become one relentless hustle, designed by A.D.D. sufferers.

A VIDEO BILLBOARD, above a building, shows a SEXY FEMALE MODEL. She smiles, then raises a hand to show a round ENHANCEMENT PATCH. Like a round band aid, similar to a nicotine patch, thick in the center, with an adhesive backing. The words TENNIS PRO are printed on the patch.

THE MODEL peels off the backing, reaches behind her head and sticks the patch on the nape of her neck.

The billboard video changes to show the model playing tennis. She handily scores against her male opponent, who looks like a pro.

Ad copy brags: TENNIS PRO... NOW YOU CAN PLAY WITH THE BEST OF THEM.

<u>EXT. L.A. STREET - NIGHT</u>
An UNMARKED POLICE CAR turns a corner and races down a side street into an INDUSTRIAL PARK.

Bland office buildings with attached warehouses. Billboards on the roofs promise paradise for the price of a patch.

<u>INT. POLICE CAR</u>
APRIL BROWN is driving. She's attractive, serious and professional.

Next to her is RICK DANIELS. A middle-aged cop. Both are plain-clothes detectives.

Rick checks the MAGAZINE of his large handgun, then snaps it back in.

                RICK
There I was, all alone in the dead end alley with six bangers coming at me. Only had two rounds left. The bangers had every kind of weapon you can imagine. Two had autos. The others: swords, nunchuks, you name it. It was like a Hong Kong flick, but I wasn't feeling like Jet Li. I was screwed.

                APRIL
So what'd you do?

                RICK
I dropped to my knees, took aim. One shot first, but missed. I blew both gunmen away. The other four saw my pissed-off face and realized they'd better not mess with me. They didn't know I was out.
                (smirks proudly)
So the suckers surrendered.

                APRIL
Almost there. You loaded?

                RICK
Yep. Explosive rounds.

                    APRIL
Explosive! ...Why?

                    RICK
Every criminal's a threat. Threats have to be
neutralized.

                    APRIL
Yeah, but, explosive rounds? This is only a–

                    RICK
                 (interrupts)
Listen, you just got promoted to detective. If you
want to be my partner, take my advice. Give them the
hard line.

                    APRIL
What about judicious force, Rick? Is that a lost art?

Rick ignores her. Takes out a SMALL METAL CASE, like
the ones for cigarettes. Opens it.

Inside: COLOR-CODED ENHANCEMENT-PATCHES.
Printed on each PATCH is a DESCRIPTIVE LABEL.

He selects one labeled MARKSMANSHIP. Peels off the
backing, slaps it on the nape of his neck.

                    RICK
When the Captain told me I was getting a new
partner, I was hoping it'd be someone with balls.

April looks out the window coldly. She pulls the car over
abruptly and stops.

                    APRIL
Getting sexist on me now?

                        11

                    RICK
        You know what I mean. I'm relying on you to watch
        my ass. Understand?

                    APRIL
        Sure. I know you'll watch mine.

That gets a slight smile from Rick.

                    RICK
        Soon as backup arrives, we're going in. You never
        know how dangerous they are, so you gotta be
        prepared for the worst.

April nods affirmative.

                    RICK (cont'd)
        Don't let me down. Our lives depend on it.

April takes out a case of her own, opens it and selects a
PATCH marked ENHANCED REFLEXES.

                    APRIL
        You won't be disappointed.

April plugs in her patch.

                    APRIL (cont'd)
        But, I don't see what you're so worked up about.
        These people are doing stuff that was perfectly legal
        two months ago.

                    RICK
        Well, it isn't now. They're breaking the law and
        we're gonna stop 'em. Got it?

                    APRIL
     Like the flu.

                    RICK
     Backup should be here any minute. Get ready.

INT. LOFT BUILDING
A class of TEN PEOPLE are standing in poses, going through
a series of punches while the INSTRUCTOR leads them. All
are dressed in loose-fitting workout clothes, future style.

The setting is a makeshift Kung Fu class. The place is actually
a storage room in the loft. Boxes are stacked tall against the
walls.

The instructor is JOHN BLAKE. He's young, athletic, serious.
There's grimness about him as if he's suffered recently.

John claps his hands. Everyone stops punching the air. They
relax while he speaks.

                    JOHN
     Good. You're showing progress. We have some new
     students, so we need to remind everyone of the
     situation.
          (beat)
     Since martial arts training is now, like guns, illegal,
     we have to keep this class a secret. The Gov doesn't
     want people to have a right to defend themselves
     anymore.

The class gives general noises of disapproval of the govern-
ment's actions.

One of them is SHINJI TANAKA, a young, tough-looking,
Asian man. His workout duds are fine-looking.

                              SHINJI
          Yeah. They wanna make sure they can stick it to us
          more easily.

Chuckles from the class.

                              JOHN
          The point is, we could all go to jail if we're caught.
          That's why I'm asking that you keep these classes a
          secret. Please don't tell your friends, your wives or
          anyone you can't trust to keep their mouth shut.

                              STUDENT
          Can't tell my wife? I don't know what's worse,
          getting busted by the cops or my old lady.

More laughter. Some guy makes a whip crack noise. The student flips him off, grinning.

EXT. KUNG FU CLASS - NIGHT
More POLICE CARS pull up. Cops pour out, weapons ready.

Rick and April get out of the car, quickly.

                              RICK
          Finally.

                              APRIL
          Where'd you get this lead?

                              RICK
          Some punk I busted for selling D.P.s yesterday. He
          told me about this class and some other stuff.

                              APRIL
          Other stuff?

                                14

Impatient, Rick walks briskly toward the entrance.

                    RICK
        Let's do it!

April and the other cops follow. Everyone starts moving
through the front doors.

INT. KUNG FU CLASS
John is finishing up his lecture.

                    JOHN
        I'm not teaching you fighting. Kung Fu is a
        discipline, which can be used for self-defense. I don't
        need to tell you how rough it can be. I've dedicated
        my life to this sport and I'm not going to let them
        take it away. Not from me. Not from you.

The students cheer. John's about to resume the class when–

–The doors burst open. Police rush in, gangbusters style.

Rick's in the lead, followed by April and the others.

                    RICK
        POLICE! EVERYBODY DOWN! ON THE
        FLOOR! NOW!

John stays where he is and raises his hands. The others notice
his manner and also remain standing.

                    JOHN
        We're not criminals, this is just an exercise class.

Rick walks up to John. The other Cops keeping their guns on
the students.

                           RICK
              Are you the teacher here?

                           JOHN
              That's right.

Rick PUNCHES John in the stomach. John doubles over.

                           RICK
              Wrong! I'm the teacher now. And when I tell you to
              get on the floor, you better get your ass down.

Shinji sees a bad situation and notices an unguarded rear entrance. He palms a patch.

                           RICK (cont'd)
                         (to the room)
              Now get down on the floor, all of you or the real
              lessons are going to begin.

All hell breaks loose. Students try to escape every which way.

Most of the Cops wield nightsticks. They lay into the students with them.

The students try to defend themselves using what little martial arts they know. Fights break out all over.

John and Shinji run behind a high stack of boxes at the rear of the room.

April whips out a gun. Gives chase.

                           APRIL
              HALT! POLICE!

But John and Shinji disappear before April can finish her sentence.

She runs behind the boxes and finds a door leading to a dark hallway.

She catches a glimpse of the two fugitives down near the end of the hall, racing around a corner.

INT. DARK HALLWAY
John and Shinji have turned a corner and are rushing down a side hall, which is dark and gloomy. The noise of the fighting recedes as they look for an exit.

Suddenly, John sees one. Double fire doors leading outside.

                         JOHN
          There!

But the FIRE EXIT BURSTS OPEN and MORE COPS charge toward them.

John and Shinji turn, open a door to their immediate left. It leads to STAIRS.

INT. STAIRWELL
They race up, the Cops hot on their heels.

April shows up and follows the Cops.

TWO COPS, aiming guns, catch up to John and Shinji.

                    LEAD COP
          ON THE FLOOR, YOU SON OF A–

Shinji spins, kicks the Lead Cop in the face.

The Lead Cop flies back into the other and they tumble down the stairs.

The Cops behind them are blocked for a second. It's all the time John and Shinji need.

They shoot up the stairs till they come to an EXIT DOOR leading to the roof.

KPOW, KPOW! Cops take pot shots at them up the stairwell. Bullets ricochet off the walls and rail.

John tries the door. It's locked.

                    APRIL
          Stop shooting! They have nowhere to run!

The door is metal. John kicks it and it doesn't budge. The Cops are coming up the stairs fast.

                    JOHN
                 (to Shinji)
          Are you crazy? You don't hit a cop!

                    SHINJI
          Us or them, bro!

                    JOHN
          But now they're trying to kill us!

The sound of approaching Cops gets louder. He sees they're only a floor or two below now.

                    JOHN (cont'd)
          Christ! Hold on!

John steps back and kicks the door near the lock. It dents.

Shinji joins him and the door swings open just as April and the Cops are right below them on the next landing.

John and Shinji LEAP through the portal and SLAM the door behind them.

The Cops start firing. Bullets pass through the door, just missing John and Shinji.

EXT. ROOFTOP-NIGHT
John and Shinji stand outside the door, on either side, waiting. Cops kick it open and pour through.

John and Shinji attack, fists and legs flying. Guns go spinning through the air, kicked from hands.

The men's ferocity and skill overwhelm the Cops. April tries to get onto the roof but Cops fighting John and Shinji block the door.

John's the better fighter. He takes out two Cops in rapid succession.

Another Cop deflects Shinji's attack and throws him against a wall. The Cop whips out a BATON.

John leaps to Shinji's defense and kicks the baton from the Cop's hand, then knocks him cold.

John and Shinji look for a way out. There's none. GIANT VIDEO WALLS block access to the roofs on either side. The back sides face them, towering over their head.

                              SHINJI
          Shit!

John points at one of the walls.

> JOHN
>
> That way!

> SHINJI
>
> What?

> JOHN
>
> Trust me. Drop kick with me. Ready?

> SHINJI
>
> (beat)
>
> OK... Go!

They run toward the video wall. Jump, feet first, together.

April bursts onto the roof with Cops behind her. But John and Shinji are already flying at the wall, yelling.

> SHINJI (cont'd)
>
> Banzai!

They smash through and come out the other side, creating a big hole where a sexy model's mouth is.

Sparks, shrapnel, John and Shinji eject from this hole. They fall toward a ROOF below, flying over a steep drop to a narrow alley in between the buildings.

They hit the roof, roll and come up fast.

April has reached the hole, sees them running across the roof to the other side. She points her gun at them.

> APRIL
>
> STOP!

John and Shinji just run like hell.

April pushes the Cops aside. Shoves her gun in her shoulder holster.

                         APRIL
         Outta the way!

She backs up, then rushes at the large hole the men made, dives through head first, flying across the gap, falling to the roof.

She hits it like a pro, rolls and comes up.

John and Shinji have already leapt to another roof next door and are climbing over the opposite side. Not leaping this time.

April backs up. Determination colors her face. She runs, jumps across the gap. She makes it, barely.

April races toward where John and Shinji clambered over the edge. Sees a DRAIN PIPE running down the side of the building.

A DARK ALLEY'S below. It's empty. But April catches a glimpse of Shinji running around a corner.

                         APRIL
         Damn!

April climbs over the side and makes it down the PIPE, drops when she's several feet from the GROUND.

She runs out of the alley and finds the streets all but deserted except for a HOMELESS MAN. She looks around, gun ready. No sign of them.

April approaches the bum.

                    APRIL
        Did you see two men running this way?

                    HOMELESS
                    (spaced)
        There are no humans. Only robots. Robots!

April storms off. The bum smirks behind her back, obviously toying with her.

INT. KUNG FU CLASS
Rick and the Cops have beaten the students into submission. They're lying on the floor face down.

A Cop takes their group picture. One Cop has a metal PATCH CASE. The case is labeled: RESTRAINING PATCHES. He slaps them on the necks of the students.

Once a patch is in place, the student becomes docile.

April enters and sees the bloody state of the students. A look of mild disgust passes over her face for a second before Rick calls her name.

                    RICK
        April! Where the hell'd you go?

                    APRIL
        Chasing the teacher and another student. They
        got away.

                    RICK
        I heard shots. What'd you do, miss them?

                          APRIL
          That wasn't me. That was backup.

                          RICK
          Figures.

Rick digs through the students' belongings. Many had GYM
BAGS with them. He searches through one and comes up with
a handful of DRUG PATCHES.

                      RICK (cont'd)
          So you still think these people are harmless, April?

Rick holds out his hand. It's brimming patches.

                      RICK (cont'd)
          D.P.s.

                                        DISSOLVE TO:

A TABLE
The table has PILES OF DRUG PATCHES, like something
out of a police display on the news.

Each pile has a card label under it saying what kind they are.
You have names like: EL LOCO, HYPE, BIG MAN, SEX
MACHINE, FREAK OUT. Each patch has a lurid cartoon on
it representing the style of the drug.

                      NEWSCASTER (O.S.)
          Some call them E-Drugs, some call them D.P.s…
          Drug Patches. Whatever the name Electronic Drugs
          have become the Nation's number one problem.

PULL BACK TO REVEAL:

FEMALE NEWSCASTER

                            23

Behind her, images appear to illustrate her points. At the moment, we see the pile of PATCHES from the previous shot, reduced.

> NEWSCASTER
> Since the neural interface was invented ten years ago, brain-enhancing enhancement-patches of every kind have exploded onto the marketplace.

The display behind her changes to show a medical symbol, the Hippocratic staff with an enhanced picture of a patch next to it.

> NEWSCASTER (cont'd)
> First, there was the medical patches which help our bodies cure themselves by regulating our metabolism.

The image behind her changes to a CLOSE-UP of an open PATCH CASE with the labels on each patch.

The labels read: FRENCH, HIGHER MATH, AUTO RE-PAIR, SPANISH, JAPANESE, PHYSICS.

> NEWSCASTER (cont'd)
> Then, came the skill patches. Which made knowledge instantly available to the user's brain.

The image now shows a long line of people going around a block, waiting to get into a building with a sign that says: NEURAL INTERFACE CLINIC.

Cut to the inside of a clinic. A doctor approaches a patient sitting in something like a massage chair, with their back to the doctor. The doc presses a small device to the nape of their neck. There's a click and the operation is over. That fast.

NEWSCASTER (cont'd)
When the cost of the neural interface started
dropping, it became the most popular consumer
product in history. Nearly everyone lined up for the
simple operation.

Another PATCH CASE flashes to view. This one has labels
that read: CLASSIC LITERATURE, CLASSIC MOVIES,
FANTASY V.R., SCI FI V.R., PORN V.R.

NEWSCASTER (cont'd)
The patch products got more advanced.
Entertainment patches took movies to the virtual
level. Any reality could be bought for the price of a
rental.

Another PATCH CASE appears behind her. Now the labels
read: HAPPINESS, SERENITY, JOY, PATIENCE, HUMOR,
SENSUALITY, ROMANCE.

An ATTRACTIVE COUPLE appear on the screen and each
plugs in a PATCH. They immediately become amorous, first
smiling, gazing into each other's eyes, then making out pas-
sionately.

NEWSCASTER (cont'd)
When mood patches first appeared, the dams broke.
Now, an estimated 95% of the population has the
interface. With these patches, you can alter your
mood in a matter of seconds. Crime and divorce rates
dropped to the lowest levels in 100 years. It looked
like a golden age was about to begin for mankind.

The screen image changes to the sinister silhouette of a gangster.

NEWSCASTER (cont'd)
But that was not to be. Crime organizations, lead by
the Multi-Gang Combine, used their ties to offshore
manufacturers to develop highly addicting patches.
With only the life of an hour, these patches make you
feel superhuman.

The screen displays several people in hospital beds. Some are
tied down. Each looks like junkies going through withdrawal.
Scary. Some are rocking forward and backward, simultaneously zoned out and in pain. Like freakish zombies created by
a mad scientist.

NEWSCASTER (cont'd)
They also have a negative effect on the user's
emotional stability. An E-Drug addict becomes
immune to mood patches and develops a serious
dependency, not unlike the Crack addicts of the late
20th century.

PULL BACK TO REVEAL:

BARRED WINDOW OF AN ELECTRONICS STORE
The Newscaster is on every TV in the window. They are all
flat units that can be hung on a wall, like a picture. Rectangu-
lar HDTV screens, even thinner than the ones today.

NEWSCASTER (cont'd)
And the 20th Century street pusher has once again
become a common sight on our corners.

WIDER ANGLE-SIDEWALK IN FRONT OF STORE
A STREET PUSHER with a shoulder bag is watching the
show through the store window. He smiles at the last bit.

PUSHER
Hear that.

A GAY COUPLE walks past. The Pusher turns. He tries to hustle them but they ignore him.

                    PUSHER
          Hey, boys, I got what you need. Talk to me.

A BLACK LIMO pulls up. The Pusher takes notice and walks over to it. His demeanor changes from jaunty scumbag to re-spectful bottom feeder.

The passenger window in the back rolls down. The man inside is blocked from view, as he hands an envelope to the Pusher.

                    KANZAKI
          Special Delivery.
                    (beat)
          These are mood patches. The latest model. We want
          to see how they sell. No charge, too.

The Pusher takes the envelope and gives the mystery man his best shit-eating grin.

                    PUSHER
          I'm on it.

The window closes and the limo drives off.

MOVING SHOT-MATTE
The limo sharks through the bizarre streets of future L.A. It turns corners and heads toward a WALLED, GATED COM-POUND.

In the compound is an ASIAN STYLE MANSION. Beyond it we can see the ubiquitous video billboards on buildings in the distance. The gates open and the limo drives in.

EXT. LOS FELIZ - KANZAKI'S MANSION - NIGHT

The limo pulls into a driveway, past a fantastic Japanese Garden with Koi ponds, and up to the mansion. Armed guards are everywhere. Some have attack dogs on leashes. The dogs have modifications. Implants in their head like radio antennas.

The limo parks behind three other limos.

A guard opens the passenger door, and the mysterious limo man gets out. He's a striking ASIAN MAN in his mid-thirties. Well tailored in the fashion of his time. He wears confidence like an after shave. His name is JO KANZAKI.

The guard bows to him.

> GUARD
> Good evening, Mr. Kanzaki, sir.

Kanzaki ignores him and walks toward the front doors of the mansion. GUARDS open them.

Kanzaki passes through a hallway lined with medieval Asian armor and weapons.

INT. BOARDROOM

The room is vast. The walls covered with giant Japanese art prints. These are in fact, flat, wall-sized video screens.

In the center of the room is a large table spread with a bizarre feast. Many different kinds of International delicacies are arranged there, colorfully like Iron Chef entries.

Three men sit at the table at different points, eating casually. They are:

JORGE DIAZ: a paunchy, tattooed Mexican crime boss. With his mean face and diablo beard, he looks like Buddha's evil twin. Two Chicana bimbos sit near him, attentive.

DONNY CHOW: a stylish fellow. Fashionable in a club sort of way, without being too obvious. Very cool and suave. CHOW takes occasional hits from a shot glass filled by a fey looking young man who stands him to one side. This is Chow's ASSISTANT/BODYGUARD. He's dressed to show off his buff body. But he acts like an attendant. Keeping quiet and serious.

DUKE JACKSON: sixtyish, black and indomitable. His clothes are Africanesque, but the colorful nature of the duds belies a serious man. He doesn't look happy to be here. No bimbos for him. He's all business. He's flanked by two stern-faced bodyguards, looking like future gangsta rap warriors.

Kanzaki enters the room.

                    DIAZ
        It's about time, Jo! What the fuck, you makin' us
        wait like this?

                    JACKSON
                  (disgruntled)
        Yeah. Why you late for your own meeting? We all
        got business.

                    CHOW
        Give him some face, Duke. I'm sure he'll have some
        interesting words.

                    DIAZ
        Better be interesting. My time is money, man.

Kanzaki takes his place at the head of the table, supremely assured. Ignoring the words, he pours himself a glass of SAKE and raises it in a toast.

                    KANZAKI
          Gentlemen, here's to our enemy. He won't be with us
          much longer.

The Combine Lords look at him, surprised. There's a pregnant pause.

                    JACKSON
          Is that so?

                    DIAZ
          What do you know that we don't?

                    KANZAKI
          Let's just say I've come up with the perfect solution
          to our problem.

Kanzaki looks at the women and bodyguards, meaningfully. The bodyguards and attendants take this as their cue to leave the room.

Kanzaki picks up a remote control and points it at one of the walls. Pushes a button.

The wall art disappears and becomes TV static. The sound of TV static fills the room from well-placed hidden speakers.

ANGLE ON-BLANK VIDEO WALL

                    KANZAKI (O.S.) (cont'd)
          It's like this...

                                        DISSOLVE TO:

INT. SUBWAY TUNNEL
The sound of static becomes the sound of a subway train moving down the tracks. The train comes toward us.

INT. SUBWAY TRAIN
John and Shinji sit in an almost empty car. John looks depressed.

> JOHN
>
> It's over. I'm dead.

> SHINJI
>
> Wake up, John! They didn't kill us.

> JOHN
>
> Yeah, but they'll track us down. Now I'm a felon!

> SHINJI
>
> Any of those students talk, we'll take care of them. Don't worry. You won't do time.

> JOHN
>
> That's not the point, Shinji. I wanted to get my life together. Now I'm worse off than before.

> SHINJI
>
> So move away. Ever been to Seattle? Nice trees up there.

> JOHN
>
> Yeah, and it rains all the time. Besides, I'm broke. That class was going to pay my rent. Now I can barely afford a burger.

John looks out the window, angry.

JOHN (cont'd)
Should've got the money in advance.

SHINJI
Why are you hurting? Can't you do something else?

JOHN
I've spent my life mastering Kung Fu. All I ever
wanted to be was a teacher. It took me years to save
up the money to start a business. But, as soon as I
made one, that terrorist attacked the President. They
made martial arts illegal and wiped me out
financially. I can't get a decent job 'cause I wasn't
trained for anything else. My girlfriend left me. My
landlord's threatening to kick me out. Need I go on?

The subway car stops at a station. The doors open. John and
Shinji get up to leave. There's a bit of silence until they exit
the car.

SHINJI
I hate to say this, man, but you're being a victim.
I mean, it's us against them. The Gov's eating up the
little guy. You like being a bitch?

INT. SUBWAY STATION
They're riding an ESCALATOR that heads up to the street.
Lining the walls on either side are FLAT VIDEO SCREENS
advertising a variety of products, including MOOD and
SKILL PATCHES.

JOHN
What do you suggest? I become a gangster, like you?

SHINJI
(amused)
Me? A gangster? I'm just a club owner.

                    JOHN
You know what I mean. I'm not like you. I'm a guy
who wants to make a living doing what I love.

                    SHINJI
                (amused)
So am I.

                    JOHN
Thanks for trying to cheer me up.

They exit the SUBWAY STATION where it lets out on the
street.

EXT. STREET - NIGHT
Pedestrian traffic is sparse. A large video screen displays various ads, mostly for patches. Every other ad shows the
MAYOR OF LOS ANGELES, who seems to be a likable figure. He's smiling and waving. The sign says: ENJOY L.A.

                    SHINJI
Listen, John. My people sent me to your class to see
how good you are, and I'm impressed. We'd like you
to come work for us... instructing our associates.
We'll pay you more than you could ever have made,
even as a legal Sifu.

                    JOHN
You want me to teach gang members martial arts?
I'm in enough trouble as it is. I don't want to get
mixed up in that stuff.

                    SHINJI
Then why'd you let me into your class?

                              JOHN
          Because we were friends in high school. I like you,
          Shinji... even if you are a crook.

Shinji chuckles, then starts to leave in the opposite direction.

                             SHINJI
          Think about it, John. We can protect you from the
          heat. You'll have a grip of money before you know
          it.
                    (beat)
          But don't think too long.

John watches Shinji exit, thinking. Behind John, the VIDEO
BILLBOARD displays an ad for happy patches. The ad
reaches the end where it shows a HAPPY PATCH in gigantic
CLOSE-UP.

                                              CUT TO:

IMAGE OF HAPPY PATCH
The PATCH without ad copy. This is one displayed on a video
screen.

                         KANZAKI (V.O.)
          What you see is an ordinary Happy Patch. The kind
          everyone uses to get in a good mood.

PULL BACK TO REVEAL:

INT. BOARDROOM
Kanzaki stands before a VIDEO WALL SCREEN with his
remote control, addressing the other Combine lords.

He's very cocky and self-assured, like he knows something.

KANZAKI

My tech people have come up with a variation that
looks exactly the same. A variation that'll solve our
little problem for us.
(beat)
I call it: Devastator.

JACKSON isn't impressed.

JACKSON

OK, now... you've made a mood patch that we're
supposed to slip to him. And... it'll kill him? Is that
right? Shit! There's no way to guarantee he'd use it,
even if we could get it to him. And I know that would
be a major bitch and a half right there.

DIAZ

Duke's right. That plan's loco. We need to
concentrate on our territory. We can't off the
cabrone. He's too powerful. Now, my people got the
barrios locked! That's gold, man.

CHOW

We have to do something. This war is becoming too
costly. Maybe some kind of truce, perhaps?

JACKSON

Truce? With that asshole?

Chow yawns at the boorish statement. Gives Jackson the cold
shoulder. Looks at Kanzaki. Kanzaki expected this response
and was ready for it.

KANZAKI

Devastator isn't for the enemy. It's for a total
stranger.

The Combine Lords look surprised.

                         JACKSON
          Say what, now?

                         KANZAKI
          Devastator's going to make the perfect assassin.
          Someone the cops'll label a "lone nut."

                         JACKSON
                    (frowning)
          How's that?

Kanzaki pauses for effect.

                         KANZAKI
          You know about the skill patch. You know about the
          performance patch. But have any of you heard of a
          ninja patch?

                         DIAZ
          Ninja Patch?!

Kanzaki has them hooked. He starts to reel them in.

                         KANZAKI
          Imagine something that combines all the features of a
          skill patch and a performance patch with an added
          bonus.
                    (beat)
          It contains an Artificial Intelligence. An A.I.,
          programmed to do whatever we want.
                    (beat)
          Like kill our enemy.

EXT. STREET - NIGHT
The same Pusher is still standing in front of the same TV
store. John Blake walks toward him. The sidewalks are nearly
empty of pedestrians.

The Pusher sees John.

                    PUSHER
          Yo! You're lookin' down. How'd you like to be up?

John ignores him, walks right by, then stops.

                    JOHN
          Got any mood patches?

                    PUSHER
          Mood patches? Don't waste your time. I got
          some stuff that'll make you fly!

                    JOHN
          I just want a Happy patch. If you don't have one...

John starts to leave.

                    PUSHER
          Yo! Hold on!

The Pusher digs through his BAG quickly and comes up with
the ENVELOPE Kanzaki handed him earlier.

                    PUSHER (cont'd)
          I'm a walkin', talkin' Walmart, yo.

John turns and looks at the Pusher. The Pusher looks around
furtively for the heat.

PUSHER (cont'd)
How many you want?

John takes a step toward the dealer.

JOHN
Just one.

PUSHER
That'll be ten, chief.

John pauses for a moment, unsure. Then pulls out his WAL-LET and looks in it woefully. He's really light on money. Only a couple ones.

He pauses, then fishes out a PLASTIC CARD. The dealer pulls out a small cell phone. Punches in 10.

John waves his card at the phone. A cha-ching sound comes out of it.

The Pusher hands John a PATCH.

PUSHER
Later.

John takes the patch, puts it in his coat pocket and continues on his way. The Pusher watches him leave.

Behind the Pusher, on the myriad TV screens in the store window, a victim is being shot in the chest in some crime movie.

The VICTIM falls to the floor, dead.

The screen FADES TO BLACK.

INT. BOARDROOM
Jackson is unimpressed with Kanzaki's presentation.

> JACKSON
> Now, despite my profession, I'm an educated man.
> I read a lot. Matter of fact, I know some things about
> this technology shit. So, let me say that your idea
> sounds interesting. But it's flawed. And seeing how
> you have wasted enough of my time...

Jackson starts to get up.

> KANZAKI
> What's wrong with my plan?

> JACKSON
> What's good with it? Patches don't control people.
> Their effects are temporary.

> KANZAKI
> Not this one.

Kanzaki points and clicks his remote at the wall screen. A cartoon image of a man appears on the screen. CARTOON MAN's brain is displayed as a cutaway. Like in those old Pepto-Bismol ads where you could see someone's stomach.

The CARTOON MAN slaps a patch at the back of his neck and radio signals (shown as animated lightning bolts) go from the patch to the brain, turning the brain RED.

The letters A.I. appear in the brain after this happens. Kanzaki narrates.

> KANZAKI
>
> We put the patch on the market and some poor fool
> buys it, thinking it's a Happy Patch.
> > (beat)
> When he slaps it on, the A.I. erases his mind and
> takes over his body.

Now the animation shows the CARTOON MAN with a determined expression.

He goes out and kills people with his bare hands. His actions are almost superhuman.

> KANZAKI (cont'd)
>
> At this stage, he's ours. The A.I. enhances his body's
> physical capabilities by boosting his metabolism, and
> it gives him the skills of a trained assassin.

The CARTOON MAN works on a computer. Then changes the wiring in an alarm box.

> KANZAKI (cont'd)
>
> Our killer will have a mind as fast as a computer,
> with the skills to crack any security system.

The CARTOON MAN sneaks past cartoon guards in a high-security compound.

> KANZAKI (cont'd)
>
> He'll be able to evade guards like a high-tech ninja,
> allowing him to get straight to our target.

The CARTOON MAN reaches the private room of a politician or rich man, his VICTIM. He kills the victim swiftly and violently. The screen becomes splattered with blood, then turns solid red.

KANZAKI (cont'd)
Where he'll solve our little problem.

DIAZ
You talk a good talk, Kanzaki.

Diaz pauses to take a swig of beer.

DIAZ (cont'd)
I'm just not buyin' it.

Kanzaki waits patiently for Diaz's bombshell, guessing what's coming, but acting coy. The others look at Diaz, interested.

DIAZ (cont'd)
When they catch the killer, see, they'll be able to trace him to us. And then it's adios muchachos. Because not only do we get the whole gang SWAT coming down on our mutual asses, maybe we also get the fucking federales. I don't want to dance to that tune. I got enough migraines.

KANZAKI
How are they going to know he's ours? We won't know him.

CHOW
They'll make him talk. He'll give 'em leads.

KANZAKI
Ah...but they won't. I left out one thing.

Kanzaki smiles.

                    KANZAKI (cont'd)
          As soon as our killer finishes the job, or if he's ever
          captured... the patch fries his brain.
                    (beat)
          He'll be dead before he hits the ground.

At this last statement, all the Combine Lords seem pleased.
They laugh at, what to them, is a funny joke.

                    JACKSON
                    (grudgingly)
          Clever. I gotta admit.
                    (beat)
          So when do you plan on giving these patches a test?

Kanzaki clicks the remote at the wall screen. It returns to an
image of a Japanese tapestry.

                    KANZAKI
          Tonight.

They look at him, surprised.

                    KANZAKI (cont'd)
          I gave some to a dealer on the way over here.

Kanzaki pours himself a glass of SAKE and raises it in a toast.

                    KANZAKI (cont'd)
          Here's to the Devastator. May it be the answer to all
          our problems.

INT. PEDESTRIAN TUNNEL-NIGHT
John walks through a badly lit tunnel that passes under a major
street. He hears a couple of young men tittering ahead, as if
they just heard a sick joke.

He slows down and walks quietly, making his way to a bend in the tunnel that's blocking his view of what's going on.

THREE YOUNG PUNKS are standing over a BUM sitting on a stack of cardboard he's using as a mattress. The bum has something in the palm of his dirty hand he's eyeing with caution.

>   PUNK 1
> That's right, fresh off the racks. A buzz bomb just for you.

>   BUM
> This ain't used?

>   PUNK 1
> Told you it wasn't. You calling me a liar?

>   BUM
> No, but I ain't interested in jackin' no used patch.

>   PUNK 1
> Put it in, old man. You want to party or not?

The homeless man looks wary, but he senses they will do worse to him if he doesn't.

Before he makes up his mind, John steps into the scene.

>   JOHN
> Leave him alone.

>   PUNK 2
> What's this?

The punks walk over to John, cocky and amused. They stop a few feet from him.

Punk 1 whips out a KNIFE.

                    PUNK 1
        You gotta pay the tunnel toll. Let's see it!

John tenses up, as if ready for something.

                    JOHN
        I'd run if I were you.

All three punks laugh.

                    PUNK 1
        Ooo! Frightening!

                    PUNK 2
        Hope you like to bleed, bitch!

The Punks whip out various weapons from KNIVES to NUNCHUKS and advance on John.

Punk 1 tries to stab him, but John moves with lightning speed, grabs Punk 1's knife arm, forces it to one side.

The knife stabs Punk 2 as he attacks John with a BASEBALL BAT. Punk 2 screeches and backs away gripping a bloody wound.

Punk 3 comes in with nunchuks swinging. John hits him with few swift kicks and punches, then steals the nunchaku. Punk 3 hits the floor.

Punk 1 throws his knife at John. He dodges.

The knife stabs into John's coat pocket, sticks for a split second, then falls away. His quick movement prevented it from penetrating his body. But it cuts his clothes.

John spins, swats Punks 1 in the face with the sticks. Punk 1 hits the floor, out.

John rushes over to the bum, who's OK, smiling a toothless smile.

> JOHN
> How you doing?

> BUM
> Those guys were scary, man.

The bum starts to put the patch on his neck.

> JOHN
> Hey! I wouldn't trust that.

But it's too late. The bum puts it in.

> BUM
> S'OK. I need all the help I can get, man. You got some change?

Suddenly, the bum's eyes go wide. He starts screaming and jerking spastically. Foam comes from his mouth.

John rushes over and pulls the patch from the man's neck. He drops it, fast. It's hot and smoking.

Too late. The bum is dead.

> JOHN
> Christ...

John kicks one of the groaning punks lying on the floor.

JOHN (cont'd)

Bastards!

John leaves the punks and their victim behind. He's all fed up emotionally.

EXT. GATES CENTER - NIGHT
It's the future's version of Parker Center, LAPD headquarters. Police cars parked outside in a big lot. People going in and out.

INT. VICE DETECTIVE'S OFFICE
It's a large room with rows of desks in cubicles. Rick and April are in one, looking at photos of the arrest. Rick is pointing at a PHOTO. It's a picture of the KUNG FU STUDENTS arrested earlier. They're lying face down on the loft's floor, bloodied.

RICK

Now that's the way you take care of perps.

In the room are TWO other DETECTIVES. Both male. They're busy at their desks, pretending not to listen to the conversation between Rick and April.

APRIL

How? Beat them unconscious?

RICK

Better than let 'em get away.

APRIL

Mine were too fast. Even with a performance patch, I had trouble catching up to them.

46

                    RICK
That's why God invented the hand gun. Anytime a
perp hits a cop, you're authorized to shoot 'em. We
have to lay down the law to keep the streets safe.

                    APRIL
Just because their lawyers can't sue police anymore
doesn't mean we have to act like the Gestapo.

                    RICK
Wake up, April. This is 2019! The gangs almost took
L.A. ten years ago. We can't let that happen again.

                    APRIL
          (sighs)
I need a cup of coffee. Want some?

                    RICK
No. I want a partner who doesn't freeze up.

April walks away to the break room. Stops. Looks over her
shoulder and says:

                    APRIL
     Maybe if you start acting warm and human, I won't
     get so frosty.

Rick stares at her as she leaves the room. The Detectives (men
and women) laugh at her zinger. Rick looks annoyed.

INT. HALLWAY
April stops before a door marked RECORDS. She enters.

INT. RECORDS ROOM
The room contains a row of booths with video monitors in
them. To one side is an ante room with row upon row of blue
DVDs stacked on shelves.

                    47

A CLERK sits at a desk in this ante room. She's operating a desktop computer. A COP sits in one of the booths, watching something on the video screen before him.

April approaches the Clerk, who looks up at her.

>   CLERK
>   Can I help you?

April shows her ID to the Clerk.

>   APRIL
>   April Brown, Vice.
>   (beat)
>   I've just been assigned as Rick Daniels' partner. He
>   wanted me to review his interrogation logs from last
>   week to yesterday.

>   CLERK
>   One moment.

The Clerk starts typing on her keyboard. A robot arm on a track goes down the rows of DVDs and pulls out one, then brings it over to the Clerk. The robot arm gets another. Drops it carefully on top of the last.

The Clerk hands them over to April.

>   CLERK (cont'd)
>   You can review them in the booths back there, but
>   they can't leave this room.

>   APRIL
>   Thanks.

<u>EXT. JOHN'S APARTMENT COMPLEX - NIGHT</u>
John walks up to his building, and up some stairs to the second
floor. It's a large complex, not too swank, not too shabby. He
looks like a wreck emotionally. This has been the worst day of
his life and it's not even over yet.

<u>INT. APARTMENT HALLWAY</u>
John starts to open an APARTMENT DOOR when he's
stopped by a LOUD VOICE.

                    LANDLORD (O.S.)
        Blake!

John turns to see his LANDLORD, a middle-aged, sour-faced
S.O.B., coming down the hall.

                    LANDLORD (cont'd)
        I hope you got my rent.

                    JOHN
        ...Uh...tomorrow would be better.

                    LANDLORD
        You told me you'd have the money tonight! Where is
        it? You're six weeks behind already!

                    JOHN
        I know! Can't we talk about this in the morning?
        I'm tired.

                    LANDLORD
        You're gonna be sleeping on the street tomorrow if
        I don't see that rent. I don't care if you're some kinda
        Karate Champ, I'll have your ass thrown outta here!

John enters his door.

JOHN
We'll talk in the morning.

The door slams shut in the Landlord's face.

<u>INT. RECORDS ROOM - VIDEO BOOTH</u>
April examines the discs she checked out. She's got a DISC
PLAYER and a VIDEO MONITOR before her in the booth.
They're old, but more futuristic than what we have now.

The video screen shows the Drug Pusher from earlier. He's
talking into the camera, looking unhappy and shifty-eyed. We
hear Rick's voice O.S. asking questions.

PUSHER
...so, this guy I know from a strip club ...uh, he's
small time. Combine, y'know. He tells me there's a
Kung Fu class next week. Says I should go. Thinks
I might learn how to protect my merchandise.

RICK (O.S.)
We'll get to that in a minute. I want to know about
this other thing you mentioned. This building in
Van Nuys.

PUSHER
(nervous)
I don't know what to tell you about that...

Rick slaps the Pusher in the face. Hard.

RICK (O.S.)
Does that make it easier?

PUSHER
Look, I...

50

Rick slaps him again.

                    RICK (O.S.)
     You were saying?

                    PUSHER
     It's dangerous!

Rick's gun comes from O.S. and points at the Pusher.

                    RICK (O.S.)
     You want dangerous? I'll show you dangerous.

                    PUSHER
     OK! OK! There's some talk I overheard among
     the, you know, the connected types. Anyway, they
     said some Combine cat hired some bangers to watch
     the place. It's in a Mex gang zone, so no one goes
     near anyway.

                    RICK (O.S.)
     And?

                    PUSHER
     They're supposed to smoke anyone who tries to
     enter. Weird, huh? I mean, it's not holding anything
     important from what I've heard. It's like they're
     expecting someone to show up there.

                    RICK
     Who?

                    PUSHER
     Hell if I know. My data's purged, chief. You got the
     whole download.

                              RICK (O.S.)
So where is it?

                              PUSHER
It's a warehouse on Cohasset. Uh... 9670.

                              RICK (O.S.)
OK, back to this Kung Fu class...

April stops the video. She takes a note pad and writes: "9670
Cohasset, Van Nuys. Combine?"

She looks at the time, gets up and grabs the discs.

                              APRIL (sotto)
Why didn't I hear about this, Rick?

April turns off the video monitor.

INT. COMBINE SURVEILLANCE ROOM - NIGHT
A SECURITY MAN faces a video wall showing a WARE-
HOUSE. Next to the chair is a table with a phone. Standing
next to the security man is Kanzaki.

                              KANZAKI
Anything?

                              SECURITY
Not yet.

                              KANZAKI
Keep your eyes glued to this screen. I'll have
someone relieve you in four hours.
                    (beat)
If anything happens in front of this building, I want
you to call me no matter what. Understand?

SECURITY
Yes, sir.

KANZAKI
Good. Because your life depends on it.

Kanzaki leaves the room. The Security Man learns forward and watches the screen more intensely, looking mighty nervous.

EXT. APRIL'S APARTMENT BUILDING - NIGHT
It's similar to the apartment buildings one can find on the Westside in these times, but there is a slightly futuristic look to the place.

A car, April's, pulls into the gated driveway.

INT. APRIL'S APARTMENT
A homey, but modest abode, tastefully decorated. Pictures on the wall show April with her father and mother. A picture of a big hound that must have been the family dog at one time. A picture of a small girl hugging the dog. The picture was taken in the late 1990s when April was a little kid.

April enters and turns on the lights. She throws a small stack of mail on a table by the door.

She walks across the room and picks up a phone by her couch. She pulls a note out of her purse and looks at a phone number written on it.

Next to the number, the words: SURVEILLANCE SERVICE. She dials.

The phone doubles as an answering machine. There's a SMALL VIDEO SCREEN built into it.

A WOMAN'S FACE appears on the PHONE SCREEN. The woman has a police uniform on.

                    FLETCHER
          Police Service. Officer Fletcher.

                    APRIL
          Hi. I'm Detective April Brown, Narcotics.
                    (shows her ID)
          I asked for a video stakeout on a warehouse in
          Van Nuys.

                    FLETCHER
                    (looks O.S.)
          Let me check the log... hmm. Yeah... our crew
          installed a hidden camera across the street. It went
          on line an hour ago.
                    (faces front)
          We encountered some gang members. Seems like
          they're guarding the area.

                    APRIL
          Is someone monitoring it now?

                    FLETCHER
          Yep. We'll call your mobile number when they spot
          anything unusual.

                    APRIL
          Thanks. Bye.

After hanging up, April hits the messages button. The readout
says: 1. Rick's face appears on it.

                    RICK
          April, Rick. I can't say we had the best first day on
          the job but I'm willing to give you a chance. Just

RICK (cont'd)
remember, I'm your superior and I'll be reporting
your performance to the Captain come review time.
I hope by then your attitude has improved.

The message ends. April takes a deep breath.

APRIL
I love this job already.

She looks at the message readout which now says zero messages.

APRIL (cont'd)
I've gotta get a social life.

April starts taking off her work clothes and heads for the bedroom.

INT. BLAKE'S APARTMENT - NIGHT
It's small and neat. Along one wall are some shelves with trophies and PICTURES. The furniture is nice, but cheap.

John has changed into a black tee-shirt, black jeans and sneak-
ers. He sits on the couch, reading a magazine, bored and unhappy. An empty beer bottle sits on the coffee table before
him. John picks up the bottle, notices it's empty. He gets up,
heads for the kitchen.

As he passes the shelves, he looks at his trophies and pictures.
One of them shows John in a Kung Fu outfit, proudly holding
a trophy. Another shows him with his arm around an attractive
woman. His girlfriend from happier times. She has a vague
resemblance to April. Same hair style.

He grabs that PHOTO and stares at it, sadly. Sets the photo
face down on the shelf, turns to go to the kitchen.

But something catches his eye. His jacket, thrown over a chair. He picks it up and examines the damage caused by the muggers. It's been ripped. He sighs.

The knife stabbed his jacket pocket. There's a puncture there. He reaches in the pocket and pulls out the PATCH. He tosses the jacket on the couch. Looks at the patch.

                    JOHN
          Damn!

The patch's been scratched. He examines it closer.

                    JOHN (cont'd)
          Might still be good.

John looks around the room again, at the trophies, photos, the face down picture of his girlfriend. He sighs, depressed. He looks at the patch one more time, then puts it on the back of his neck.

John tenses up suddenly, surprised... in PAIN.

The room goes RED, BLUE, all sorts of colors. Everything distorts around him. The furniture and walls seem to be changing shapes. Then blackness descends.

He falls to the floor. Unconscious.

                              FADE OUT.

INT. JOHN'S APARTMENT- DAY
Sunlight streams through the curtains. John is still lying on the floor, out.

A BANGING sound is coming through the FRONT DOOR.

LANDLORD (O.S.)
Blake! Open up! I want that rent!

John doesn't stir. There's more banging. Then it stops. A
SOUND OF JANGLING KEYS replaces it.

LANDLORD (O.S.) (cont'd)
Get ready. He's some kinda Chop Sockey dude.
If he tries anything...

EVICTOR 1 (O.S.)
I hope he does.

The door opens and the LANDLORD enters with THREE
HUGE MEN. They look like professional bouncers. All
glance around, looking for trouble. One of them spots John on
the floor.

EVICTOR 1
That him?

LANDLORD
What the hell...?

Evictor 2 moves up to John.

EVICTOR 2
Looks like he got ripped and passed out.

Evictor 2 kneels by John, starts to lay a hand on his shoulder
to roll him over. John's eyes open. Alert.

Suddenly, John rolls over on his own. He punches Evictor 2 in
the chest. Evictor 2 is lifted up by the punch, then falls gasp-
ing to the floor.

John swiftly rises before the other Bouncers react.

The Landlord and remaining Evictors see that Evictor 2 is coughing blood.

                    EVICTOR 3
         Doug!

They look at John with mixed anger and horror. John's expression is strange, cold and calculating in an almost inhuman way. He stands with an obvious readiness to do more damage.

The remaining two Evictors attack. John moves with blinding speed and disables them.

The Landlord almost wets his pants. He backs away from the advancing John.

                    LANDLORD
         Uh... look, John... maybe... Maybe I can give you
         more time.

John shoves the Landlord out of the way. His expression, cold and mechanical. He leaves the apartment without looking back.

The Landlord gets off the floor, goes to the phone and dials 911. A static image of a face comes up on the phone. A generic 911 operator.

                  PHONE (recording)
         911 Emergency. Please Hold.

The screen goes blank, then flashes the words: PLEASE HOLD. YOUR CALL WILL BE ANSWERED IN THE ORDER IT IS RECEIVED. In English, Spanish, Japanese and Korean.

LANDLORD
Shit!

INT. SUBWAY STATION - DAY
John enters the subway station. The walls have video billboards in them playing commercials. The languages change
each time they play. The place is quiet except for the distant
hum of a subway car leaving. A few people are listlessly
waiting for the next train.

Blake looks around like someone appraising a situation. His
face is a calm mask. He walks by a bank of billboards. Between each commercial a video of the MAYOR appears. That
happy, go-lucky guy we saw earlier. He's smiling and waving
at us from the BILLBOARD while a female voice says:

NARRATOR
Mayor Strazewski wants you to have a nice day in
beautiful L.A.!

John stops and watches the ad. His hands go up to his head as
if he feels a sharp pain there. He staggers to a bench and sits
down. Some commuters notice his behavior.

John stares back at the commuters with obvious confusion on
his face. A TRANSIT COP looks at him, then pulls out a palm
top computer.

John blinks and rubs his eyes, doing a double take at the world
around him.

CUT TO:

JOHN'S POV - SUBWAY STATION - SAME
COMPUTER READOUTS appear around the bustling commuters. TARGETING POINTS on their bodies' are indicated
for maximum lethal effect. The patch is telling him the best

ways to kill everyone. When INFO pops up around someone, it reveals whether they are carrying a gun or knife. He looks at the Transit Cop across the room.

The Transit Cop stares back, then looks down at his computer, which is pointed at John, like a camera phone.

A readout appears next to the cop that indicates the cop's GUN in his holster. The words: POTENTIAL THREAT appear.

TRANSIT COP'S POV - SUBWAY STATION

On the Cop's computer screen, John's face is displayed in real time. It freeze frames it. The cop hits a button and the word: TRANSMITTING appears.

INT. SUBWAY STATION

John's confused, dazed. He stands up. Goes into the MEN'S ROOM nearby. The Transit Cop is joined by a SECOND TRANSIT COP.

INT. MEN'S ROOM

John enters, walks over to a sink and looks at himself in a MIRROR. He doesn't recognize himself.

INT. SUBWAY STATION

The two Transit Cops look at the computer as a photo of John Blake appears on it. It's his driver's license photo.

John's name and address appear below. Then the words flash: OUTSTANDING WARRANT. Charges are listed: ASSAULTING A POLICE OFFICER, RESISTING ARREST, UNLAWFUL ASSEMBLY, TEACHING MARTIAL ARTS.

The cops draw their guns and head for the Men's Room. Transit Cop 2 speaks into a RADIO WATCH.

                    TRANSIT COP 2
        547 to base. We've spotted suspect John Blake
        at Sunset Station. Send backup.

                        RADIO
        10-4.

INT. MEN'S ROOM
The door opens and John sees the reflection of the Transit
Cops entering with grim expressions and weapons drawn.

                    TRANSIT COP 1
        Hands on the wall. Now!

John spins and kicks Transit Cop 1 in the stomach, knocks
him back into Transit Cop 2. They collapse in a pile.

As fast as that happens, John leaps over their bodies, and races
away.

Transit Cop 2 can't get a shot off, because John's out of sight
before he can recover.

INT. SUBWAY STATION
A SUBWAY TRAIN starts to leave the station. With an inhuman leap, John lands on its roof. He lies flat on the surface.

The train speeds away down the tunnel.

INT. MEN'S ROOM DOORWAY
The Transit Cops scramble to get up, but Transit Cop 1 is in a
lot of pain. Transit Cop 2 calls for backup again.

                    TRANSIT COP 2
        547 to base. Suspect has fled the scene! We have an
        officer down! Needs medical attention!

He looks around for their attacker, but John Blake is gone.

<u>EXT. PEDESTRIAN SUBWAY – DAY</u>
April and Rick are on the job, talking to a UNIFORM COP.
The subject of the conversation: The dead homeless man John
ran into the night before.

> BEAT COP
> He was found this morning by some kids.

> RICK
> A Jacker.

> BEAT COP
> Looks that way.

April turns the body over slightly. A burn mark on the nape of
his neck. The patch is on the ground where John dropped it,
discolored and curled as if it had been hot.

> APRIL
> Don't they know used patches might blow out
> and kill them?

> RICK
> They're bums. What do you want? They dig through
> trash and use what they can find. A lot of them think
> they can jack the patches before they blow. You see
> this stuff a lot when you're working Narco. Get used
> to it.

> APRIL
> I thought no one jacked anymore. Too risky.

> RICK
> Well, we've been finding more of them lately and–

Rick's cell phone rings. He answers.

                    RICK (cont'd)
          Excuse me.
                    (into phone)
          Yeah? No kiddin'? We're on it.

He puts the phone away. Turns to leave the alley, gestures that
April follow.

                    APRIL
          What's up?

                    RICK
          Remember that Kung Fu bust? Looks like the
          instructor went nuts. Assaulted his landlord and two
          transit cops.

They rush back to their car, parked on the street nearby.

EXT. JOHN'S APARTMENT COMPLEX - DAY
Police have arrived on the scene and are questioning the
LANDLORD outside the apartment. The Bouncers are being
carted off on stretchers by AMBULANCE CREWS.

                    LANDLORD
          And I hit him a couple times but he grabbed me
          before I could nail him. Then he threw me across
          the room!

April and Rick show up on the scene. They approach the cops
and the Landlord. Rick flashes his ID.

                    RICK
          Detective Daniels, Vice. This is my partner, April
          Brown. We heard there was an assault here.

COP

Yeah. Some guy took out three professional rollers. The landlord witnessed the whole thing.

LANDLORD

His name's John Blake and he owes me rent! Don't kill him till I get my money!

INT. JOHN'S APARTMENT

April and Rick enter the APARTMENT. They see BLOOD STAINS on the carpet. April goes to the shelves and picks up the photo of John with the trophy. The Landlord hovers by the doorway, looking in.

APRIL

Rick.

RICK

What?

APRIL
(shows photo)
It's definitely him. Our boy from last night. But didn't you put out a warrant on him?

RICK

Yeah. Warrants always takes a couple days to act. Back log.

Rick notices a PHOTO laying face down on the shelf. He picks it up. It's the photo of John's ex-girlfriend. April is looking around the place.

APRIL

This doesn't look right to me. I don't even know this guy and already I get a sense this isn't like him. Kung Fu teachers should have more discipline than that.

Rick shows the picture to the landlord.

> RICK
> You know her?

> LANDLORD
> Yeah, that's his ex-girlfriend. I overheard the whole
> "let's be friends" speech a couple weeks ago.

Rick puts the picture down.

April takes out a palm computer and keys in John Blake's
name. She then hits a menu selection that says: A.P.B. and hits
the SEND key. The words: A.P.B. CONFIRMED appear on
the LCD screen.

EXT. STREET-DAY
John comes out of a SUBWAY entrance and looks around. He
sees a MAN getting into his car. John approaches swiftly, but
in a manner that doesn't draw attention. With one blow, John
knocks him out.

He gets in the car and drives off. The man is left lying on the
street.

EXT. STOLEN CAR - DAY
As John drives, the reflection of the WAREHOUSE is on the
windshield. John's expression is very determined.

INT. CAR - SAME
The warehouse is not before him, just the 101 Freeway, North.
What we saw before was his imagination.

He's driving through traffic. He has no idea what this warehouse is, but it's on his mind in a big way. Like a ghost image
it keeps flashing before him.

                    JOHN (sotto)
          Van Nuys...Warehouse...
                    (beat)
          Why...? What's there?

John pulls over. His face becomes screwed up with pain and
confusion. His hands are shaking.

                    JOHN (cont'd)
          What's wrong with me?! Why can't I remember
          anything?

He bangs his head on the steering wheel. The glass still shows
a reflection of the Warehouse. A ghost image, an image that
he can't avoid. He becomes determined again.

                    JOHN (cont'd)
          Whatever's happened...
                    (beat)
          Answers in the building.

He pulls out into traffic again.

<u>EXT. KANZAKI'S MANSION - DAY</u>
A limo enters the long driveway. CHOW and his male assistant exit the car when it stops. Gardeners are working on the
well-manicured lawns and shrubs.

<u>INT. KANZAKI'S OFFICE</u>
Inside the mansion somewhere. It's spacious and extremely
well-decorated. A ultra-modern layout with bizarre art and
black leather furniture. Kanzaki is behind his DESK, paging
through items on his COMPUTER.

Suddenly, his secretary buzzes him on the INTERCOM.

KANZAKI

Yes?

SECRETARY (O.S.)
Mr. Chow's here to see you, sir.

Kanzaki squints, wondering what this is about.

KANZAKI

Send him in.

Kanzaki turns to face the door. It opens and his SECRETARY ushers in Chow. Chow's assistant waits outside. The Secretary closes the door.

CHOW

We need to talk.

Kanzaki motions to the couch. Chow sits.

KANZAKI
What can I do for you, Donny?

CHOW
Duke Jackson doesn't like this plan of yours.
He's going to use it to bring you down and
Diaz's backing him.

Kanzaki gets up and goes to a cabinet.

KANZAKI

Drink?

CHOW

Often.

Kanzaki smiles, gets a bottle and two glasses. He pours for both of them, then returns to his seat.

                    KANZAKI
          Duke's old. Born in the '60s. He doesn't like young
          blood or young ideas. I don't expect he'll last long.

                    CHOW
          That's why I'm here. You can win with my help. We
          can take over the others' territory. And the enemy's.

                    KANZAKI
          We've been friends a long time, Donny. I don't
          forget my friends.

                    CHOW
          Neither do I. That Diaz's a pig. And Duke... how he
          nailed the old gangs is a legend.
                    (beat)
          But even legends die.

                    KANZAKI
          I already know Duke's looking to eliminate me. But
          that's not really why you're here... is it?

                    CHOW
          Mm.
                    (beat)
          It's just that...I see a couple flaws in your plan.

                    KANZAKI
                    (smiles)
          Oh?

                    CHOW
          What if it gets removed? Won't the effects wear off?

KANZAKI

The patch won't allow the user to take it off. He's
possessed. And no one will get close enough to take
it from him.

CHOW

So what if the user has a weak body? They'll only
become as strong as a healthy person. Or what if your
patch gets bought by a cripple, or an old lady?

Kanzaki smiles and deliberately puts a distance between
Chow's question and his answer.

KANZAKI

Devastator has an unique advantage.
(beat)
What do you know about Ninjitsu?

Chow raises an eyebrow.

CHOW

Only that there haven't been any real ninjas in over
100 years.

KANZAKI

But Ninjitsu itself. The art of the Ninja?

CHOW

Well... that's all a secret, passed down from
generation to generation, by the ninja orders. It's not
something you can learn on the street.

Kanzaki nods, waiting for Chow to say more.

CHOW (cont'd)

And... uh, those orders are families. You have to be
born into one to learn their arts.

KANZAKI

So... if there were a modern individual who was descended from a line of ninjas and knew their secrets...

CHOW

They could put those secrets on a skill patch?

Kanzaki lets a moment lapse, then–

KANZAKI

It was said that ninjas could become invisible, that they could cast illusions and kill with one blow of their hand. Imagine someone with all those skills and with amped-up muscles. Strength and agility beyond those of regular humans.

CHOW

OK, fine. But my question remains. What if your patch was bought by a cripple or a weakling?
A failed assassination is going to make the enemy extra-hard to clip.

Kanzaki points his remote at a WALL SCREEN. The image of the WAREHOUSE seen earlier appears.

KANZAKI

First, the patch makes the user show up at this uninhabited warehouse. Inside he finds out who he's supposed to kill. Before that happens, he has to get inside. That's how I'll know if they're effective.

CHOW

You've got people watching it?

                    KANZAKI
    Expendable people.

                     CHOW
                   (laughs)
    This I've got to see!

                    KANZAKI
    My service should call me as soon as the action
    starts. You're welcome to a ringside seat.

ANGLE ON-VIDEO SCREEN
The picture of the Warehouse is displayed.

EXT. STREET IN FRONT OF WAREHOUSE-DUSK
John's stolen car pulls up some distance away and parks. He
gets out, looks around. He spots several CHICANO GANG
MEMBERS (Cholos) hanging around the area, watching him.
They start to approach, menacing.

John takes an appraising look. Gets back in the car and drives
off. The Gang lets him leave, shouting taunts and obscenities
his way. Some throw bottles.

Time passes.

EXT. STREET IN FRONT OF WAREHOUSE-NIGHT
John's car returns. The gang members take notice and start
yelling taunts.

The car lines up with the front of the warehouse where the
Cholos have parked their wheels.

These gang cars are a nightmare blend pimped-out lowriders
with future-tech wackiness. Neon trim. Video doors showing
cartoons and Mexican wrestling.

John's car just sits there, a safe distance from the Cholos, pointed at them as if waiting for something.

The Cholos start to walk toward it, brandishing all sorts of weapons. Some have guns.

INT. CAR

On the passenger seat, and filling up the rear of the car, are as many plastic gas cans as it will hold. A gas-soaked CLOTH STRIP leads from the mouth of one to the front seat. A BRICK sits near it on the seat. All the windows of the car are rolled up.

John pulls out a lighter and ignites the cloth. The flames lick down it like a fuse. He grabs the BRICK and jams it onto the gas pedal, then exits the car as it starts to race forward.

EXT. STREET - CONTINUOUS

The Gang sees the car race toward them.

John falls out, rolls, then moves for cover. They open fire at John and the car.

                    CHOLO 1
          Maricone!

The car comes at them like an unstoppable freight train. The Cholos leap out of the way.

KABOOM!! The car explodes sending napalm flames and flying glass everywhere. Some Cholos are fried. Some get slashed and burned. Some are running around like human torches.

The car keeps moving forward, on fire, until it crashes into the lowriders.

Flames spill out onto the lowriders and one by one they go up like cherry bombs. BOOM BOOM BOOM! Flames shoot high into the night.

The surviving Cholos pick themselves up. Some help put out their comrades. One of them runs toward the shadows between the warehouse and another building.

CHOLO 1 (cont'd)
Over there!

The Cholos chase after John.

SPLIT SCREEN - INT. COMBINE SURVEILLANCE SERVICE
At the Combine service, the security man sees the cars explode on his video screen. He picks up the phone.

SPLIT SCREEN - INT. POLICE SURVEILLANCE SERVICE - SAME
A woman assigned to watch the screen reacts to what's happening by picking up a phone to make a call.

SPLIT SCREEN-APRIL BROWN/JO KANZAKI
April's CELLULAR PHONE, a TINY DEVICE in her PURSE rings. She takes it out. Kanzaki's DESK PHONE rings at the same time. He picks his up.

APRIL
Yes?

KANZAKI
What?

EXT. ALLEY - WAREHOUSE - NIGHT
Three Cholos run into the alley between the Warehouse and a neighboring building.

The alley's deserted. John's nowhere to be seen.

The Cholos check any side doors (which are locked), and look in a dumpster. John isn't there. He isn't anywhere.

Suddenly, John leaps at them from the roof. He lands on the largest Cholo, knocking him down. He takes out the other two swiftly.

John senses something. He turns sideways and blends with the shadows, disappearing from sight, like a ghost.

Six Cholos rush into the alley and are surprised to see their fallen comrades.

CHOLO 2
What the fuck?

John appears from the shadows, behind them. He attacks before they are aware of his presence. His actions are incredible. His speed, punches, kicks and jumps reveal he has passed beyond human levels.

When he's finished, he takes a KNIFE from one of the dead men's hand.

EXT. FRONT OF WAREHOUSE - NIGHT
John, with patient menace, walks out of the alley. Only three Cholos are left. They look at him like cornered animals.

JOHN
I want some answers.

One Cholo named Ramon draws a gun and moves to shoot him.

                              RAMON

        Fuck you!

John throws the knife and it hits Ramon in the chest. He falls
back dead. The others turn and run away.

John is on them in a flash. He knocks one out with a blow to
the head. The other he throws to the ground. He puts his foot
on the man's chest and starts to question him.

                              JOHN

        Who am I?

                             CHOLO 3
                            (scared)
                  What? I...I dunno, man!
                             (beat)
                  D-Don't you?!

                              JOHN

        Why'd you attack me?

                             CHOLO 3
        Someone paid us to do whoever tried to enter the
        warehouse!

                              JOHN

        Why?

                             CHOLO 3
        I dunno! I swear!

                              JOHN

        Who were they?

                             CHOLO 3
        They were Combine. Combine guys.

                    JOHN
What's their names?

                   CHOLO 3
I dunno, man! Ramon knows! He's the one who dealt
with them!

                    JOHN
Where is he?

The Cholo looks around at bodies of his fellow gang members.
He points to the man John just killed.

                  JOHN (cont'd)
Too bad.

John punches the Cholo in the face, knocking him out. He
turns and walks toward the warehouse entrance.

EXT. UNMARKED CAR - NIGHT
April and Rick's car is racing through traffic on the 101 freeway. A bubble light has been put on the roof. It's passing
through the Valley around Studio City, heading north.

Things have changed in the next 30 years. Lots of skyscrapers
with video billboards dot the Valley. It's as crowded as the
other side of the hill.

INT. UNMARKED CAR
April's doing Indy 500 style driving. Rick's the passenger, and
he's looking surly.

                    RICK
What's the rush? Where are we going?

APRIL

A warehouse in Van Nuys. Ring any bells?

RICK

Who... told you about that?

APRIL

The other night, you said an informer talked to you
about things, but you wouldn't elaborate.
(beat)
So, I looked over your interrogation discs. The
informer mentioned this warehouse, so I had the
stakeout service watch it for me.

RICK

You what?! Christ, April!

APRIL

Something important's going down and you ignored
it. Why?

RICK

There's a lot you don't know. One thing you don't do
is get involved in Combine business. That's the Gang
SWAT's job.

APRIL

Did you report it to them?

RICK

Turn this car around. You don't want to get into this.

APRIL

Why not?

                         RICK

Gang SWAT works for the big boys. They're covert
and dangerous. We can both lose our jobs if we get in
their way. Or worse. Turn around.

                        APRIL

That's crazy!

                         RICK

That's politics. Turn this car around. Now!

                        APRIL

Too late. I've already called the L.A. County
Sheriffs, since it's their turf.

                         RICK

The Sheriffs?!
                    (beat)
You've screwed us both. I hope you realize that!

INT. WAREHOUSE-NIGHT

John's inside the gloomy warehouse. Crates are stacked up
high in places. They could be hiding someone. He scouts the
place out. No one inside, except him.

A LIGHT shines down from the ceiling in one spot. He heads
toward the light. It's illuminating an area with a BIG VIDEO
SCREEN, some CRATES OF WEAPONS and OUTFITS.

As soon as John steps into the light, the screen comes to life. It
displays a silhouette of Jo Kanzaki.

                       KANZAKI

You've made it. Excellent. Obviously the person who
owned that body was a superb athlete.
                    (beat)

                          78

KANZAKI (cont'd)

In those crates are supplies you'll need to eliminate your target.

JOHN

Who are you?

KANZAKI
(surprised)

...What?

JOHN

Who are you? Why am I here?

Kanzaki doesn't say anything for a moment. But, he remains cool. He's assessing the situation.

KANZAKI

You're not behaving according to your program. Why is that?

JOHN

I want some answers!

KANZAKI

Do you remember who you are?

JOHN

No...I...

Kanzaki smiles. Friendly, assuring.

KANZAKI

We...We need you to assassinate a criminal who's behind the E-Drug menace in our city.

                          JOHN
What's my name?

                         KANZAKI
Devastator.

                          JOHN
Who were those guys outside?

                         KANZAKI
They work for the man you have to kill.

                          JOHN
Why? Who is he?

The screen suddenly shows a picture of the MAYOR OF LOS
ANGELES. He's the same smiling, happy go-lucky fellow
we've been seeing all along, but in this photo he looks serious
and isn't smiling. He looks more like a hard-nosed business-
man. It seems to have been taken by a paparazzi, as it shows
him leaving a building.

                      KANZAKI (O.S.)
         His name's Fred Strazewski. He hides behind the
         office of the Mayor. But in fact, he's a major crime
         lord in the Russian Mob. He uses the Police Gang
         SWAT unit as a private army against his enemies.

John looks confused.

                   KANZAKI (O.S.) (cont'd)
         You should have a complete map of his compound
         in your head. Use the gear I've provided to do
         the job.

John looks down at the equipment. There is a stack of papers.
He picks them up. They're crazy looking death threats on the

                            80

Mayor's life made of pasted-up letters and doctored pictures of the Mayor with horns and 666 on his forehead. Each note calls the Mayor a tool of Satan who must be purged. There is a strange design at the bottom. And the notes are signed: The Devastator

                    KANZAKI (cont'd)
          Take those notes and tack them to the wall of your
          apartment. Keep another on you at all times. That
          way, when you kill the Mayor, the police will know
          why you did it.

                         JOHN
          The Mayor...?

                        KANZAKI
          Are you confused? Don't you know your target
          by now?

                         JOHN
          I...yeah, I understand.

                        KANZAKI
          Good. Now do your thing, Devastator.

EXT. WAREHOUSE-NIGHT
SEVERAL L.A. COUNTY SHERIFF CARS pull up. They get out, guns ready. These are the Valley Cops. They have tan uniforms as opposed to the dark blue of the LAPD.

April and Rick's CAR pull up last. The Sheriffs check out the bodies of the Cholos. The Cholo who John interrogated comes to. When he sees the Sheriffs, he points to the warehouse and says—

                         CHOLO
          There! He's in there...!

Sheriffs rush to the doors and kick them in.

INT. WAREHOUSE
John drops the notes, and turns at the sound of the police outside. The screen with Kanzaki on it goes blank. John turns back to the SCREEN.

                    JOHN
          What's going on?!

The SCREEN doesn't answer. It has been turned off.

INT. KANZAKI'S OFFICE
They're seated in his office watching the MONITOR that shows the inside of the warehouse. Chow's concerned.

                    CHOW
          What's wrong with him?

                    KANZAKI
          I don't know. Maybe he got a bad patch. Something's
          not right.

Kanzaki picks up a REMOTE. He punches some buttons on it and the VIDEO MONITOR now shows a man's face.

                    MAN
          Yes, sir?

                    KANZAKI
          We have a situation. Send a crew to the warehouse.
          Erase any witnesses.

                    MAN
          Hai!

The VID SCREEN goes back to showing the warehouse. On screen: John rummages through BOXES OF WEAPONS.

The screen flicks back and forth from that image to an outside shot of the warehouse, with bodies lying around on the ground.

                    KANZAKI
        Oh, well...Back to the drawing board.

                    CHOW
        His fighting skills were impressive. Maybe he'll
        still be useful.

                    KANZAKI
        He might have been, but this blows everything–look!

The monitor has picked up the Sheriffs as they inspect the bodies of the gang members and advance on the warehouse, guns ready. April and Rick can be seen walking into the shot.

EXT. WAREHOUSE
April and Rick meet with SIX L.A. COUNTY SHERIFFS. Rick flashes his I.D. at them.

                    RICK
            We're from Gates Center. An D.P. case we've been
            working has connections to this warehouse.

A Sheriff named CARSON takes an amused wave at the BODIES. The others draw their guns.

                    CARSON
        Well...looks like we have probable cause.

April pulls out her CELLULAR PHONE. Dials.

                    APRIL
          This is Detective Brown. What happened at the Van
          Nuys surveillance?
                    (beat)
          Where's he now?
                    (beat)
          Thanks.

April hangs up her PHONE, turns to Rick and the SHERIFFS.

                    APRIL (cont'd)
          One guy did this. He's still inside. And... he fits the
          description of John Blake!

                    CARSON
          Who's John Blake?

                    APRIL
          He's wanted for several assaults, including attacks on
          two transit cops. Not to mention holding illegal
          martial arts classes. He's extremely dangerous.

Carson looks at all the dead Cholos.

                    CARSON
          You don't say.
                    (to Sheriffs)
          Seal off all the exits!

INT. WAREHOUSE
John loads weapons into a slim BACKPACK. HANDGUNS,
AMMO, SHURIKENS, a BURGLAR'S KIT. He grabs an
odd-looking skintight suit with a strange wrestler-type mask
that has the crazy notes pattern on it. He looks around as he
loads the bag, wary and somewhat paranoid.

He puts on the pack, hears the Sheriffs entering the building. He merges with the shadows.

The Sheriffs enter the WAREHOUSE, wary, GUNS ready. April and Rick follow Carson and fan out once they're inside.

John stands in the shadows, wary. But suddenly, he acts as if he has a massive headache.

The IMAGE OF THE MAYOR OF L.A.'s face is SUPERIMPOSED over the scene. Then it fades. And John recovers, slightly shaken.

The Sheriffs are getting nearer. They're combing the warehouse, looking for John.

John leaps on a high stack of crates, as Sheriffs close in. They don't see him. They don't hear him.

April is the first to discover the cache of weapons and the video screen, now showing snow. She picks up one of the notes John dropped. Sees how whacked out they are. Focuses on the word MAYOR.

                    APRIL
          Rick, over here!

Rick comes over to see the supplies. The video screen. He looks around for Blake.

                    RICK
          John Blake! This is the police! Come out with
          your hands up!

At the sound of his name, John moves in the shadows, confused. April turns to look around, spots John briefly.

85

APRIL
          Hey! There he–

John seems to vanish in a blur. April and Rick move to where
he was a second ago, guns ready. He's gone.

EXT. STREET OUTSIDE WAREHOUSE - NIGHT
Several vans race in and screech to a halt. COMBINE MEN
leap out, sporting automatic weapons. They're mostly black.

The SHERIFFS outside reach for their guns. The Combine
Killers shoot them before they can do anything. The Killers'
guns have silencers, so those inside are unaware of what's
going on.

The LEAD KILLER is grim looking, with a scarred face.

LEADER
          No survivors.

The Combine Killers pour into the warehouse. A few others
go around the building and shoot any Sheriff they see.

INT. KANZAKI'S OFFICE
Kanzaki and Chow watch the mayhem on the video monitor.
Chow is upset.

CHOW
          Jo, are you nuts?! This'll unify all the law
          enforcement agencies against us!

KANZAKI
          Not us. The only evidence points to Duke Johnson.
          I hired some of his men, by proxy, to do the work
          without his knowledge. Duke will take the blame and
          our boy will do the Mayor proper.
                    (beat)

KANZAKI (cont'd)
Provided he escapes. Which will be a further test of his skills.

Chow eases back, relaxing.

CHOW
This is getting more interesting by the minute.

INT. WAREHOUSE
John moves quickly. The Sheriffs search the warehouse, but he always manages to evade their sight. ONE SHERIFF thinks he sees movement. He shines a light but catches nothing.

John moves toward a high window, leaping from one stacked crate to another. He reaches it.

He starts to open the window, crouching on a high crate. But then–

–The COMBINE KILLERS enter the warehouse, gunning down those close to the front door.

Only two remaining Sheriffs are left, Carson and one other. They take cover and return fire. April and Rick do the same.

John stops and surveys the action for the moment. He sees April. She's pinned down by crossfire.

April pulls out a small hand radio, to call for backup. Bullets take huge chunks out of crates near her head as she makes the call.

APRIL
1027 to base! We have a Code 3 at our 20.
Send backup!

The only sound her radio makes is harsh feedback.

                              APRIL (cont'd)
          They're jamming our radios! We're on our own!

April's partner, Rick, blasts away at some crates from where
two Combine Killers are shooting. His explosive rounds blow
massive holes in the crates, but the Combine goons are well
shielded.

                              RICK
                    Bastards!

Rick sees April's trapped nearby. But far enough that he can't
help without moving. He leaps from one stack of crates to
another, shooting wild to keep his enemies at bay.

                              RICK (cont'd)
                    Hold on, April!

John watches the whole scene with interest. But he does
nothing. His attention is drawn to April.

<u>POV - JOHN</u>
He sees April in CLOSE-UP with his newly enhanced vision.
He tenses, obviously interested in her. John shakes his head.
Then looks at the proceedings with surprise.

Rick is trying to get close to April. But he doesn't see a Combine Killer take aim at him from behind a crate.

POOF POOF POOF! Blood sprays from Rick's body in three
places as he takes rounds. He spins like a rag doll and falls to
the floor, dead.

                              APRIL
                    RICK!

Carson and the other Sheriff get nailed. April is the only one left. The Killers start to close in on her location.

KILLER 1

Say g'nite!

JOHN RISES. Intent on coming to her aid. But–

–Before he can do anything, April stands and starts firing madly at her assailants in a desperate attempt at survival.

APRIL

Good night!

She nails two Killers before the rest of them return fire in a hurricane of flying lead.

April drops to the floor and barely avoids getting hit.

KILLER 2

Suck lead, cop whore!

The Killers keep firing at where she was. Their explosive rounds blow open some of the crates above her.

The crates are full of LARGE CERAMIC VASES. Vase shards fall on April, followed by whole vases. She tries to roll out of the way.

KRASH! A large vase smashes down on her head. She's out.

The remaining Killers move in on April from several directions, guns aiming.

They're ready to empty their magazines. The leader smiles and cracks:

LEADER
Bitch wants something in her. Let her have–

SHUK! A SHURIKEN appears in the leader's forehead. He falls back dead.

The Killers turn, firing wildly in every direction.

WHUD! One of the Killers is knocked flat by a shape that flits in from the shadows, then disappears. The Killer is out cold. Only two Killers remain standing. They're scared.

KILLER 2
Fuck this!

Killer 2 pulls out a grenade from his jacket. Pulls the pin. Drops it on April.

KILLER 2 (cont'd)
See ya!

The Killers run for it. John drops from above, scoops up the grenade in one swift motion and throws it at them.

He drops to the floor covering April with his body. WADOOM! The Killers are spray.

John picks up April and heads for the front door. He kicks it open. It flies off the hinges.

EXT. WAREHOUSE - NIGHT
John swiftly takes April to the van, ignoring the bodies. He puts her inside, then hops in the driver seat and fires her up.

The van drives off into the night. In the distance, sirens wail.

EXT. LA RIVER AQUEDUCT ENCINO - NIGHT
Balboa Park still resides between Hayvenhurst and Balboa in
Encino. The Aqueduct is also still there. John has parked the
van somewhere secluded near the Aqueduct where no one can
see them.

INT. VAN
John checks April. She's still out. He has laid her on the back
seat of the van. He searches her. Comes up with her driver's
license. It has her home address on it. She lives in Silverlake.

He searches the van until he finds a plastic water bottle. It's
half full. One of those 12 oz things. He takes off the top and
shakes a little onto her face.

April sits up fast, disoriented, but reactive.

                    APRIL
          Rick! —What?!

April sees John looking at her. Reaches for her gun. Her holster's empty.

                    JOHN
          I took you away from there.

April doesn't say anything. She just stares at him. Then looks
at her surroundings, worried but trying to look brave.

                    JOHN (cont'd)
          Are you all right?

                    APRIL
          Where's my partner?

                    JOHN
          They killed him.

April puts a hand to her head. Recalls what happened.

                    APRIL
          And the others?

                    JOHN
          Dead. They almost got you, too, but I stopped them.

                    APRIL
                (cautious)
          Thanks. Are you turning yourself in?

                    JOHN
          For what?

                    APRIL
          You attacked people. Don't you remember?

John looks confused.

                    JOHN
          Back at the warehouse? They were trying to kill me.
          Kill you.

She realizes he is not all there. She tries to be cool, patient.
Like a Sunday school teacher.

                    APRIL
          No, John. I'm talking about your landlord and his
          bouncers. And the cops you attacked. Don't you
          remember?

                    JOHN
                (confused)
          John? Why did you call me John? I'm the Devastator.

                    92

APRIL

Look... come with me and I will get you some help.
It's obvious you're having some problems.

JOHN

My name is John?

APRIL

Yes. John Blake. And you're wanted for several
crimes. I'm a police officer. My name is April
Brown. I need you to come downtown with me.
So we can talk to some people who can help you.

JOHN

I thought you were... someone who could help. I need
to know more.

APRIL

I'll be happy to tell you whatever you want, but it'll
have to be downtown.

John gets tense, backs away a little.

JOHN

I don't trust you. Don't trust anyone.

Realizing this is a touchy situation, she tries to handle it by
being firm.

APRIL

John, you have to come in with me. This is not your
decision to make.

JOHN

Need to talk to the Mayor.

April thinks he's babbling so she talks to him like he's a child.

                         APRIL
         OK, John. We'll let you talk to the Mayor at the
         station.

John lashes out with his hand. A two finger jab to the side of
her neck. April stiffens, looks at him wide-eyed.

                          JOHN
         No.

He looks around to make sure no one is in sight outside.

                     JOHN (cont'd)
         You'll be able to move soon. It's just a nerve pinch.

He opens the door to the van and in a blur, disappears. April
stares at the place he was seconds ago, only able to look that
way with her eyes. She can't turn her head.

A brief amount of time passes. She starts to sweat as she
struggles to move her fingers. Slowly, she is able to curl them.
Then, move her arms and legs, slowly.

She gets up, obviously straining with all the effort of her will.
It gets easier for her as the seconds pass.

She exits the van, clumsy. She almost falls to the ground.

She stands shakily. Then starts to walk, looking around for
any sign of him. He's gone.

                         APRIL
         Damn!

April gets in the van and starts her up.

EXT. WAREHOUSE - NIGHT

The van pulls up. LA SHERIFFS are swarming all over the place with forensics teams. Coroners are hauling away body bags, loading them in the backs of vans marked LA COUNTY CORONER.

Members of the LAPD Gang SWAT are there. They are a stoic looking bunch in black armored uniforms. Spooky.

April gets out of the van, flashing her badge to get to the scene. A Sheriff Captain comes over to her. He looks annoyed. A GANG SWAT OFFICER watches them.

                    CAPTAIN
          Can I help you?

                    APRIL
          Yeah. I'm the only survivor of this mess.
          April Brown, LAPD Vice.

The Captain looks at her van.

                    CAPTAIN
          Oh? Did you decide to go to the mall while my men
          were dying in there?

                    APRIL
                (tense)
          I was abducted by the major suspect. I just escaped.

                    CAPTAIN
          So where is he?

April sighs.

                    APRIL
          Got away.

95

CAPTAIN
I thought you just got away.

APRIL
Look, Captain, this is a complicated story and I'll put it in my report.

CAPTAIN
What were you doing here?

APRIL
My partner and I were on a case. Evidence led to this warehouse. We were checking on it with the Sheriff's department.

CAPTAIN
Uh-huh. Your partner's name?

APRIL
Rick Daniels.

The Captain looks at a palm computer. Some information flashes on the screen.

CAPTAIN
Ah, yes...DOA. So were my men. And there were other bodies, too. They look like Combine thugs, but most of them are splattered all over the walls. It's making it hard to ID them.

APRIL
Who owns the warehouse?

The Gang SWAT Officer comes over to them.

CAPTAIN

We haven't checked that yet. More importantly, who's the perp you mentioned? Where did you see him last?

April sees the coroner loading dead Cholos into the van. When she looks back, the Gang SWAT Officer is eyeing her coldly.

GANG OFFICER

Detective Brown. You violated department regs with your surveillance. Your report will have to be cleared by our division. In fact, you will sign a statement we'll give you. You will stick by this at the hearings.

APRIL

Sir, there's a suspect we've been following, John Blake and–

GANG OFFICER

That will be all. You're to report back to Gates Center. Your supervisor has something to tell you. We'll finish up the work here.

The Gang Officer smiles at her coldly and turns to walk away. The Captain looks at her with a slight amount of sympathy before steeling up his expression and turning back to his men.

April watches them, stunned.

EXT. MAYOR'S PALACE - NIGHT

Looking like a classic Bel Air mansion, the Mayor's palace sits behind high walls with video cameras everywhere. Armed guards patrol the yard. A high metal gate with a guard is the only entrance to the place.

That doesn't stop John. He arrives stealthily, wearing the DARK OUTFIT that came with his gear. He has the PACK on. He puts on a MASK that came with his suit. It has a strange design on the face like the design on the mad notes he left behind in the warehouse.

John takes position behind a tree, hiding him from the video cameras on the wall. When the roving cameras are turned away, he climbs the tree swiftly.

He waits until the cameras look away again, then LEAPS from the tree to the wall in an almost superhuman fashion. It's a good ten feet of space between the tree and the wall. No problem.

He JUMPS from the wall to the backyard lawn and rolls behind a HEDGE.

A guard walks by and doesn't notice anything. John crouches in his cover and waits for the right moment to move again.

EXT. FRONT GATE - NIGHT
April's unmarked car pulls up. The guard comes over. She rolls down the window and shows him her badge.

                    APRIL
          I'm Detective Brown from Gates Center. I need to
          see the Mayor right away. It's an emergency.

                    GUARD
          Stand by.

The guard goes back to his shack and makes a call. April waits.

EXT. MAYOR'S BACKYARD - NIGHT
John moves across the yard, making sudden stops when guards are near. He blends in with the scenery. They don't see him.

He comes to a wall of the house. Above him is a BALCONY on the second floor. He leaps up, catches an edge and pulls himself up, then throws himself over the guard rail.

A guard walks by below, and looks up. He sees nothing and continues on with his rounds.

EXT. BALCONY - NIGHT
John slides a door open and moves inside the house, crouching.

INT. MAYOR'S HOUSE - GUEST ROOM #2
It's a spare bedroom. No one's inside. He looks around, then thinks.

POV - JOHN
He sees the FLOOR PLAN to the house superimposed over the real vision of the place, like a map in a computer game. This is Guest Room #2 according to his display. He moves to the door and listens. Someone's coming.

INT. HALLWAY
One of the Mayor's associates is walking down the hall. His name is GEVORK. He's a tough-looking Russian. Gevork walks past the door where John is hiding and enters a double door at the end of the hall.

INT. MAYOR'S HOME OFFICE
It's a large room. Luxuriously appointed with antique art and furniture. The style is classic European. But there are futuristic aspects to the place, as well. A stereo/video wall displaying stock figures from all the markets, news, plus surveillance of the grounds. A high-tech executive's desk with a built-in flat screen computer system.

MAYOR STRAZEWSKI walks into the scene and sits behind the large desk, following him, a hot-looking female AIDE. She has a large palm top with information flashing across the screen.

The Mayor looks at it, while adjusting his tie. The Aide's clothes look in slight disarray as if the two of them have just been up to something.

In a far corner of the room, where they have just left, is a DI-VIDER, the kind people used to dress behind. This one is very expensive. Antique.

                    MAYOR
          OK, Sheila, I want ten million put into this account
          by Monday. We'll deal with the ancillary issues next
          quarter.

Gevork enters.

                    GEVORK
          Uh...excuse me, sir.

The Mayor looks at Gevork, annoyed.

                    MAYOR
          Ever hear of knocking, Gevork?

                    GEVORK
          Sorry, sir. But there's someone to see you. A police
          detective. She says it's urgent.

The phone rings. The Aide answers.

                    AIDE
                (to phone)
          Hello?

MAYOR
(to Gevork)
I'm busy. What's it about?

AIDE
Please hold.

GEVORK
She says you're in danger and you need to be warned
about someone.

MAYOR
(annoyed)
Christ. All right. Tell her–

AIDE
(interrupting)
Sir, Conrad's on the phone about the shipment.

JOHN enters the room, and no one sees him because the
Mayor is talking to his Aide and Gevork is waiting on them
both.

John moves in such a fast and stealthy manner, he evades their
sight. He shoots quickly across the room and hides behind the
divider.

There's a small bed behind it. The sheets rumpled from recent
activity. The Aide's panties are on the floor.

MAYOR
Tell the cop to wait. I have to take this call. Make her
tell you her story.

GEVORK
Da.

Gevork leaves. The Aide goes with him. He looks her up and down. She smiles and straightens up her clothes.

John eavesdrops, and peeks through a small space in the divider so he can see what's going on.

> MAYOR
> (to phone)
> I'm putting you on screen.

The Mayor hits a button and one of his men appears on the screen.

CONRAD is a hip minion. He looks a little nervous. And the Mayor has become a lot harder.

> MAYOR (cont'd)
> Speak. What happened to my patches?

> CONRAD
> They... they said someone hijacked our shipment.
> We still haven't learned who did it. We're trying to
> find out right now.

The Mayor slams his fist down hard on the desk, livid. His Aide and man on the screen jump.

> MAYOR
> I want those patches back in 24-fucking-hours or
> I'm gonna staple your balls to the ceiling!

> CONRAD
> But, sir. We don't have any leads. The crew that did
> it were like ghosts. We–

                    MAYOR
                (interrupts)
Use your head, retard! We're dumping patches on the
market to force out the Combine! So who do you
think did it? I'll give you three guesses! Find those
D.P.s and don't waste my time until you have them!
Got that?

John looks surprised by all this.

                    CONRAD
        Yes, sir. I'll do my best.

                    MAYOR
        Your best better be good enough.

The Mayor lifts up his desk stapler and does a couple mock
staple motions to make his point. He hits a button, hanging up.
The screen returns to showing stock quotes.

John frowns. He does not like what he's heard. He reaches
into his pack and pulls out a throwing star.

His compulsion to kill the Mayor is suddenly very strong. The
scene takes on a RED PULSING COLOR for him. He starts to
stand, but someone rushes into the room. It's Gevork.

John sits down again. He puts the star in a slot on his sleeve.

                    MAYOR
        What now?!

                    GEVORK
        Sir, I got a call from SWAT. The Combine sent some
        amped-up killer after you. He's probably on his way
        here. I'm having our men search the compound.

GEVORK (cont'd)

SWAT's on the way. And the cop outside confirms
the story.

MAYOR

All right! I'm locking myself in the vault. Tell Sheila
to join me.

The Mayor gets up to leave the room. Two Security Guards
come in to search the place.

GUARD

We're just sweeping the area, sir.

MAYOR

If you find this freak, cripple him. I want
to interrogate the bastard.

One of the Guards approaches the divider.

John KICKS the divider down. Attacks the two Guards. Guard
1 goes down fast. Guard 2 takes aim.

The Mayor reaches for a gun in his desk. Gevork whips out a
big piece.

John leaps over the body of Guard 1 as Guard 2 shoots at him.
Before the shot goes off, John moves to one side, kicks Guard
1's gun off the floor.

Guard 2's shot misses John. The gun John kicked hits Guard 2
in the face, right between the eyes. He's knocked backward,
off his feet.

Gevork fires blind. John comes in low. Gets close to Gevork
before he can shoot him, knocks the gun from his hands.

Gevork seems to know martial arts. He strikes and kicks at John. John evades. Then attacks.

Gevork goes flying back into a GLASS HUTCH. Antiques shatter, glass sprays.

The Mayor shoots at John twice, missing both times as John evades, moving too fast, spinning, jumping, acting like a dervish. John whips the star from his sleeve, throws it.

SHUK. The Mayor gets it right between the eyes. He falls back, dead.

APRIL and two more GUARDS burst into the room.

                    APRIL
          John! Stop!

John pauses a second, unsure.

The Guards shoot him. Bullets hit John in the arm, chest and leg. He falls to the floor.

Guard 2 recovers, getting up. They all move in on John, aiming to kill.

In a blur, John rolls to one side, behind the desk. They can't see him.

                    GUARD 2
          Shit! He's wearing body armor. Even his head!

He moves under the desk, flips it on the Guards and April. They're knocked backward.

John crashes through a window, diving for the BACKYARD.

April and a Guard recover fast and shoot at John, but he's already through the window. Guard 3 shouts to whomever's in range.

GUARD 3

He's outside!

The Guards run out of the office in pursuit.

April checks on the Mayor. He's dead. She starts to follow the Guards, but her eye catches sight of something on the Mayor's desk.

A small control panel with a video screen, says: CALL LOG.

She looks closer. The last call has the entry – CONRAD. RE: LOST SHIPMENT

APRIL

Shipment?

EXT. BACKYARD - NIGHT
Floodlights come on, illuminating the scene. John becomes visible. Two Guards stand between John and the wall he's racing toward. They open fire.

He falls, rolls, comes up near them. With lightning speed, he batters the Guards, taking them out. Then, keeps on running toward the wall.

SPAK SPAK SPAK! Bullets chew up the lawn and the wall around him as he leaps up and catches the edge of it.

Blake pulls himself up. The Guards from upstairs are now firing at him from the backyard.

Blake takes two in the back, but doesn't slow down. He makes it over the wall.

The Guards run to the gate to chase after him.

INT. MAYOR'S OFFICE
April watches the end of the Mayor's conversation about the lost shipment. The tape only shows Conrad, but the Mayor's voice is on the recording.

April pushes a button and a tiny CD pops out of a slot in the desk. She takes it.

EXT. BEL AIR STREET - NIGHT
On the street facing the Mayor's compound, TWO BLACK VANS of the Gang SWAT pull up and unloads a SWAT team.

The leader's the same Gang Officer who spoke to April earlier. One of the House Guards runs up to them. Points to the wall.

> GUARD
> He just scaled the wall over there! He's gotta be close by.

> GANG OFFICER
> Is the Mayor all right?

> GUARD
> No. Murdered.

The Gang SWAT look at each other.

> GANG OFFICER
> (to Guard)
> We'll take it from here. Go back inside.

The Gang Officer goes to the van and whips out a cell phone. Makes a call.

In the distance, behind some bushes in another yard, John watches the scene with interest.

The Gang SWAT aren't doing anything. Just standing around waiting for orders. The Leader talks into his radio.

John moves on, staying low, keeping covered. When he's in the clear, and out of their range, he runs off into the night.

<u>EXT. STREET - NIGHT</u>
April's car pulls out of the compound gates. She stops when she sees the Gang SWAT vans and cops. The SWAT's getting back in their van.

The SWAT Officer sees April's car and walks over. She rolls down her window.

                         APRIL
          You sure get around.

                     GANG OFFICER
          I thought I told you to report back to your supervisor.

                         APRIL
          I was on the way, but I decided to stop by and warn
          the Mayor about Blake.

                     GANG OFFICER
          You could have called.

                         APRIL
                    (sarcastic)
          Yeah. But you never know who might be listening.

April drives off before he can respond.

EXT. BEACH - NIGHT
John runs along the beach. It's night, but flashes of color impinge on his vision. It becomes a green day, a blue night, a yellow day. John is tripping, his eyes are wild. He looks panicked. And he's followed by hallucinations. Ghost people appear around him. Kanzaki races with him, along side.

KANZAKI
You're Devastator. Devastator. Devastator.

John stops. He punches at the ghost, pained. The ghost disappears. His Landlord appears as a ghost next to him.

LANDLORD
Where's the rent?! The rent! The rent!

John kicks at the ghost. It disappears. John puts his hands to his head as if it hurts horribly. He moans.

IMAGES flash in his mind as his memory starts going berserk. He sees a mixture of images around him. The background disappearing. The scenes are in vivid color while he is a gray shadow in the midst of it.

FLASH: The class is busted by the cops
FLASH: The subway ride with Shinji.
FLASH: Shinji: We want your services...
FLASH: The happy patch he bought from the dealer.
FLASH: The fight in the tunnel.
FLASH: Kanzaki telling him to kill the Mayor.
FLASH: The Mayor talking about e-drugs.

Realization crosses his face. John reaches to the nape of his neck and finds the drug patch there. He pops it out. Looks at it, surprised.

109

JOHN

Well now...

Suddenly, the patch flashes in his hand. He drops it. It lays smoking in the sand.

He looks around. Shakes his head as if he's trying to get over double vision or some hallucination. He puts his hands to his head, as if in pain.

JOHN (cont'd)

What did they do to my head? AH!

More memory flashes around him—

FLASH: Kanzaki tells him to kill the Mayor.
FLASH: He sees the patch is scratched after coming home.
FLASH: The Mayor shouting in the phone about the Combine.
FLASH: Shots of his childhood: learning martial arts, seeing his first Jackie Chan flick. His first date.
FLASH: His girlfriend dumps him.
FLASH: His conversation with April in the van.
FLASH: Kanzaki: You're our best agent.
FLASH: Landlord: The rent's due!
FLASH: April: You're a wanted man.

Again and again, the visions play, faster and faster until he drops to his knees and screams.

He stops. He sits there, looking at the ground, his eyes averted from us. He breathes deep. Becomes calm. He looks up. His expression, fierce. There's fire in his eyes.

Now he knows who made the Devastator patch. Who sent him on the kill. And why.

It's payback time.

EXT. STRIP CLUB - NIGHT

As if the zoning codes were thrown out years ago, this section of town looks like an acid trip designed by ad men and porn merchants. Neon everywhere. Colored lights dancing and flashing. Projected images zooming across the ground and up walls. Noises, music, booming base. People yelling at each other. And this is OUTSIDE!

In the midst of this visual mayhem is a STRIP CLUB that puts the other buildings to shame. The main sign says: PUSSY GALORE. A neon chick in a cat suit with cat ears winking at us. Garish signs next to the entrance scream: NUDE SEX BOMBS INSIDE.

GIANT HOLOGRAPHS of DANCING NAKED WOMEN are projected from the roof, but the private parts are hazy due to computer editing.

A CAB pulls up. John gets out, mask off, but wearing the suit. He looks around, wary.

He walks into the club, like a sheriff in a Western, headed for the final showdown.

INT. STRIP CLUB

John walks through the bizarre scene. Virtual holo strippers and the real thing dance it out in the wide, wild club. Lasers flash across the room. Pounding music rams the beat into the patrons. Neon flickers in the darkness.

As strange as his costume is, it's not any weirder than what the customers are wearing. John moves toward the back, up some stairs that lead to an office that overlooks the club floor.

A large BOUNCER bars John's way at the top.

                    BOUNCER
This area's private.

                    JOHN
I'm here to see Shinji.

                    BOUNCER
He's busy.

John slashes out with his hand, hitting the Bouncer in the side of the neck with two fingers, just like with April earlier. The Bouncer stiffens and starts to fall forward. His eyes wide open in surprise.

John shows his advanced strength by keeping him from falling down the stairs. He forces the paralyzed Bouncer down, making him sit on the floor.

                    JOHN
You'll be OK in a few minutes.

John leaves the scene, entering Shinji's office.

The Bouncer sits with his eyes wide open, sweat trickling from his brow.

INT. SHINJI'S OFFICE
It's like something a Japanese Pimp might think is cool. Tiger-skin wallpaper. Nude paintings of women in fluorescent paint framed by neon. Leather couches. A couple Japanese art pieces are out of place in all this. A money cat sits on a shelf.

A wall-mounted flat screen is playing. Shots of the Mayor before and after John met him flash by. A picture of John, last seen in his apartment, is now gracing the 11 O'Clock News. No volume, the pictures speak loud enough. He's a wanted man.

Shinji is getting blown by a club girl on the couch. His eyes closed, he's floating on cloud nine.

He opens his eyes and spots John standing there. Shinji reacts surprised, shoves the girl and starts doing his fly. His girl looks at John.

> SHINJI
> Shit! What the fuck?! John!

> JOHN
> Hiya, Shinji. How's pimping?

Shinji tries to be cool now.

> SHINJI
> Whatever. What are you...

He looks at John's outfit. The mask is tucked in his belt.

> SHINJI (cont'd)
> Nice threads. I hear you're wanted now. Welcome to the crime club, Dillinger.

John gently grabs the girl's hand, leads her out of the office and shuts the door behind her.

He turns to look at Shinji and his eyes are all business. John's intense. Scary. But he's holding it in. We can feel the angst coming from every pore.

> JOHN
> I'm not here to socialize. I want some info.

Shinji leans back in his chair, trying to be casual. But he's a little nervous. After all, his homeboy here just smoked the Mayor according to the news.

SHINJI

What am I, the Internet?

JOHN

You know what I need to know.

SHINJI

About what?

JOHN

Your bosses.

SHINJI

Did you miss the neon titties outside? This isn't a
comedy club.

JOHN

You work for the Combine, Shinji. I want to know
where the bosses are.

SHINJI

What's the matter with you? You know I can't tell
you that! Besides, you couldn't get to them, anyway.
Take a friend's advice and–

John grabs Shinji by the front of his shirt and slams him back
into a wall. His face becomes a demon's mask.

JOHN

I don't care if you and I were friends! My life's
taking a nose dive into the abyss because of them!
Where are they?!

Shinji sees there's no point in keeping it from him. He's
scared by the new John.

                         SHINJI
OK, OK! Be cool. Don't freak on me.
                    (beat)
The man you're looking for's named Kanzaki. He has
a Japanese style castle in Los Feliz. Go up Western,
north of Hollywood Blvd, and you'll see it up on the
hill. Can't miss it.

                          JOHN
Why'd he want the Mayor killed?

                         SHINJI
Competition. When he got elected, the Mayor turned
part of the police into a machine to crush his rivals.
Then he took over their business. Only the Combine
was smart and powerful enough to survive. But he's
turning his guns on them. Get it?

                          JOHN
Warn them and I'll kill you.

Before Shinji can say anything, John seems to disappear right
in front of him.

The door to the office slams shut, making Shinji jump. He
grabs a bottle of Tequila on the table, pours himself a shot.
Slams it. Exhales.

INT. VICE DEPT. SUPERVISOR'S OFFICE - NIGHT
April is standing in her boss' office. He's reading some papers
as if she isn't there. He puts them aside and looks at her. Hard.

                          SUPER
You're suspended pending a full inquest. Hand over
your badge and your gun.

April's stunned.

                    APRIL
        Hold on! I've uncovered major leads regarding the
        Mayor's assassination and that bloodbath at the
        warehouse. You can't suspend me now!

                    SUPER
        Watch me. Now hand over the gun and badge.
        I won't ask you a third time.

Silently, April does what he asks. She puts the gun and the
badge on his desk.

                    SUPER (cont'd)
        You'll be summoned when the papers are filed. Go
        home and start typing a resume. You'll need it.

                    APRIL
                (seething)
        I can't believe this. You're just going to let these
        gangsters run this town?

The Super decides to humor her one last time.

                    SUPER
        For your info, Lieutenant, the Gang SWAT has taken
        over the case. It's their bailiwick, not yours. If you'd
        turned over your info on John Blake from the
        beginning, your partner and a lot of L.A. County
        Sheriffs would still be alive.

He lets that sink in. April looks a little wounded.

                    SUPER (cont'd)
        This isn't the Wild West. We're a team and when you
        buck the system, you're playing against your peers.

He goes back to reading his paperwork.

                    SUPER (cont'd)
          Now go home.

April turns to leave. She stops just as she's opening the door.

                    APRIL
          You became supervisor after the Mayor was elected,
          didn't you?

The Super sneers. His expression confirms our suspicions about him.

                    SUPER
          Have a nice day.

April leaves. As she walks through the department, the eyes of many detectives are on her. She clenches her fists. Determination hard on her face.

INT. APRIL'S APARTMENT - NIGHT
April enters, hits the lights and drops some mail on a table by the door with her keys.

Suddenly, she reacts surprised to something she sees O.S.

John is sitting on her couch. He's been waiting for her. Once again dressed in that costume. Mask off, in his lap.

April reaches for a gun, instinctively, then realizes she doesn't have one anymore.

                    JOHN
          I'm here for help.

APRIL

How did you get in...?
(beat)
Never mind. How do you know where I live?

JOHN

Your driver's license. When you were unconscious.

April's wary.

APRIL

Why did you come to me?

JOHN

I need to clear my name. I can't do it alone.

APRIL

You murdered the Mayor, John. I saw it. There's
nothing to clear. You're an assassin. I'm a witness.
(beat)
And you want my help?

John stands. April tenses. He tries to reason with her.

JOHN

It wasn't me. Not like you think. I used a happy patch
they altered somehow. It messed with my mind.
Made me want to kill the Mayor. But something was
wrong with it. I was able to gain control of my
thoughts. I took it off just before it tried to fry my
brain.

APRIL

When did you use it? The patch, I mean?

JOHN

Back at my apartment. After I came home from the bust. I was depressed. So I bought the patch.

APRIL

Can you prove any of this?

JOHN

I threw the patch away. It was fried. But I know where we can get proof.

APRIL

Tell me.

JOHN

A Combine Lord's home. His name's Kanzaki. The patch may have fried, but I was left with all the talents it gave me. I know I can sneak in there and get what I need. But I don't have much time. I need someone in the law to take my side when I present my case.

April is quiet for a moment. Wheels obviously in motion inside her head.

APRIL

I need help, too.

John sticks out his hand. Smiles.

JOHN

Partners?

She takes it.

APRIL

In crime.

EXT. KANZAKI'S MANSION - EARLY A.M.

A road leads up to a security gate. Beyond that is Kanzaki's castle. It's walled off on all sides. Outside the compound, the once stately area is no longer free from garish video billboards. There are several near the compound, turning slowly, displaying commercials for patches.

April's car drives past the road leading to the gate. It parks on the cross street.

John and April get out. They look around, warily; then, April pops the trunk. Inside, a small ARSENAL.

April dons a bulletproof jacket. She puts two guns in shoulder holsters. She packs mucho clips in the bandoleers of her jacket.

Then she pulls out patch case, selects the patch for MARKS-MANSHIP and puts it on her.

John does a similar routine, puts on his mask. Takes what weapons are left from his Ninja arsenal. He activates his suit's stealth mode by touching a button on his arm guard.

An LCD screen says: STEALTH ACTIVE

> APRIL
>
> What's that do?

> JOHN
>
> Makes me invisible to infrared alarms and motion detectors.

> APRIL
>
> Cool toys.

JOHN

The only thing they gave me that's worth a damn.

They turn and walk toward one of the walls. John makes a small grappling hook appear in his hand, almost like magic. A cord is attached that runs to a reel in his suit somewhere.

He throws the hook at the wall's top, and it catches. He makes it up the wall in no time. April follows, more slowly.

John helps April up. He doesn't spot TWO GUARDS on the other side of the wall who see them.

John and April drop over the side, and find themselves looking down the barrel of two machine guns.

GUARD 1

Bad news. Halloween's over.

GUARD 2

The ground. Face down. Hands behind your heads.

John drops to the ground, but throws two SHURIKEN STARS in the process. The guards fall backward, dead.

John and April drag their bodies into the bushes.

APRIL

Got to be more careful. I want to get through this in one piece, you know.

John looks a little worried.

JOHN

Those instincts the patch gave me... they're fading. We better move fast.

They rush to a wall of the house. John puts a small device on a window. The lock on the window unlatches.

A green LED light comes on the device. John puts it in his pocket and slides the window open.

April enters the window first, followed by John. They slide it shut again and duck just as a guard comes by outside.

INT. BOARDROOM
Kanzaki is holding another meeting with the Combine Lords. All are in attendance. Their bodyguards present as well. No bimbos, though.

                         KANZAKI
          Thanks for coming. The Mayor's death affects us all.
          We need to discuss the future.

INT. HALLWAY
John and April steal their way down a hall. They hear Kanzaki talking in the distance. They move toward the sound—a murmur.

INT. BOARDROOM
Kanzaki talks. The ceiling is high and paneled above him.

                         KANZAKI
          The future of Los Angeles belongs to the Combine.
          L.A. is open territory now and no one stands in the
          way.

INT. HALLWAY
John and April come on the two double doors to the boardroom. They're closed. But a door leads off to the side.

John cautiously opens it.

INT. SECURITY ROOM
TWO GUARDS are watching video monitors. They don't notice John until it's too late. He swiftly takes them out.

April joins John in the room. The monitors show scenes from around the compound, but not the boardroom. April starts pushing buttons.

> APRIL
> Let's see if we can hear what's going on.

But their attempts to spy on the boardroom fail.

> JOHN
> We're going to have to find another way.

INT. BOARDROOM
Duke confronts Kanzaki, angry.

> JACKSON
> You've put the us all at risk, Kanzaki!

> KANZAKI
> How's that? Only we know the score.

> JACKSON
> Wrong! There's some Narco bitch investigating the case. And a bunch of my men have turned up dead in a warehouse. You wouldn't know anything about that?

> KANZAKI
> No. But we can kill this detective. Throw things off.

> JACKSON
> No. We kill you! It's over.

KANZAKI
(amused)
Yes. Yes it is.

Duke signals and his bodyguards shoot Kanzaki's men, then move in on Kanzaki.

Kanzaki remains cool. Duke smiles coldly. Nods at the corpses of Kanzaki's men.

Duke's men take aim at Kanzaki. He remains calm. Even smiles as if waiting for the punchline.

JACKSON
I never thought you were clever. Now I know you're just plain stupid.

Duke begins to signal for his men to fire, but–

–Suddenly, ceiling tiles fall to the floor and with them, SIX MEN in black techno-weave costumes, like John's costume. TECHNO-NINJAS.

The Ninjas' flash swords and kill Duke's and Diaz's men with lightning-fast precision. Something is strange about these killers. They have a cold, inhuman way about them.

Duke and the others are stunned, though Chow remains calm. Kanzaki smiles at Duke.

KANZAKI
I had problems with the first trial of my Devastator, so I took the liberty of testing them further on some volunteers. Hope you enjoyed the demonstration.
(to Duke)
What were you saying just now?

Duke is too surprised to answer. Diaz is sweaty.

                    DIAZ
          Hey, Jo, I'm not in with Duke, man. I'm with you.
          That was some righteous shit!

                    KANZAKI
          Ah, yes. It's over.

The Techno-Ninjas kill Diaz and Duke with quick slashes of
their swords. The bodies fall over, spraying blood. The Ninjas
avoid the gore, wiping their swords clean.

Chow claps theatrically.

                    KANZAKI
          They even stole one of the Mayor's shipments earlier.
          That's how you get good help these days. You make
          it.

The two bosses chuckle.

INT. SECURITY ROOM
John and April have climbed onto the tables and have moved
aside ceiling tiles. They pull themselves up into the ceiling and
move across to where the boardroom is.

INT. CRAWLSPACE
John notices ceiling tiles missing in the direction they are
headed. They cautiously move toward these holes and look
down. They see carnage below. Kanzaki pours wine in two
glasses, hands one to Chow.

INT. BOARDROOM
Kanzaki chuckles. Looking at his dead colleagues. Chow remains poker-faced. But a glimmer in his eye suggests he is
also amused.

                    KANZAKI
          Now that we've eliminated the competition, let's
          celebrate with a toast.

                      CHOW
          You know, I–

Before Chow can finish, a NINJA throws something at the
ceiling.

Ceiling tiles are broken and bodies come falling through. John
and April.

John lands like a cat. April less gracefully, but unharmed.

The NINJAS move in. A fight breaks out.

John holds his own, but does not succeed in putting them
down fast.

April shoots one, but another grabs her, disarms her and puts a
blade to her throat.

                      NINJA
                   (to John)
          Submit.

John is forced to surrender.

                    KANZAKI
          Fancy meeting you here, Devastator.

                      JOHN
          The name's John.

KANZAKI

Well, John. Thanks for killing the Mayor. You've
done me a great service. Even though your patch
appears to have malfunctioned, it's the results that
matter.

JOHN

Enjoy it while you can.

KANZAKI

I intend to. And now it's time for your reward.

Kanzaki signals for his men to kill them. But before they take
action–

–BOOM! The doors blow in.

A GANG SWAT team leaps in firing guns. Four Ninjas fly
back, spritzing blood.

John dives across and gets April on the floor where they will
be safer.

Two surviving Ninjas leap up, flipping through the air,
throwing shurikens at the SWAT men.

The SWAT men deflect the stars with their guns, using them
as shields.

The Ninjas close in, but are no match for the SWAT men. The
Ninjas are killed swiftly.

When it's over, four SWAT men are standing over the dead
bodies of six Ninjas.

Kanzaki, unharmed in the fray, is looking at them completely
in shock.

John and April start to get up from the floor. The SWAT team casually walks across the room toward them. Kanzaki looks at Chow. Chow smiles and stands, then looks to the SWAT team.

> CHOW
> Good work, men.

He looks at Kanzaki. Smiles.

> KANZAKI
> These are... yours?

> CHOW
> Mm. Thanks for eliminating the others. I was planning to do it myself, but now you've provided me with a worthy scapegoat.

Kanzaki is stunned.

> KANZAKI
> Chow... what is this?!

Chow's amused.

> CHOW
> Did you really think the Mayor was his own boss? The Mayor? Who do you think financed his election?

Kanzaki, John and April react surprised.

> CHOW (cont'd)
> I was running him the whole time. He was a front for my operations. Now that you've complicated matters, the Deputy Mayor will do just fine. I own him, too.

JOHN

The SWAT team... they're not normal, are they?

CHOW

My operatives learned of Kanzaki's patch over a year ago. We stole the plans and made some improvements. These men have a more advanced Devastator patch.

KANZAKI
(stunned)

More advanced?

CHOW

They have free will, because I need them for later. But the talents are better. I've added even more killing skills. Additional espionage knowledge. And their agility and strength enhancements are far superior.

APRIL

SWAT works for you? They worked for you the whole time?

Chow smiles.

KANZAKI

So it was you waging war on the Combine! Not the Mayor!

CHOW

Competition irritates me. It's a minor character flaw, I'll admit. But there you are.

JOHN
(to Chow)

So you're the one I should be killing today!

                    CHOW
I'm afraid it's not that simple.

                    JOHN
We'll see.

                    CHOW
                  (smirks)
Ah, but I'm afraid I haven't delivered the punchline
yet. You see, you're about to do Kanzaki, then turn
yourself in for slaying the Mayor and the other
Combine lords. My men will escort you to the station
where you will make a full confession.

                    JOHN
Right. And you're going to put on a dress and sing
"God Bless America."

Chow smirks. One of his men produces a patch.

                    CHOW
We have a persuasion patch that will make you do
whatever I want. Including the murder of your friend.

Chow indicates April.

                    JOHN
Leave her out of this!

                    CHOW
                  (chiding)
Come now. I can't have witnesses.

SWAT 2 moves in on John, fast. He fights him, but SWAT 3
and 4 leap from behind and grab John by the arms.

SWAT 1 pulls out a patch and walks toward him with a mean grin.

                           SWAT 1
              Relax. This won't hurt a bit.

SWAT 2 keeps an eye on Kanzaki.

April, unnoticed, sees a gun on the floor nearby. Sees a dead ninja's sword near her foot.

She puts her foot under it, kicks it toward the SWAT 1. It flies through the air, whacks him across the back of the legs, cutting him. He turns, surprised.

John uses the distraction to break free of his captors, jumping so they are forced back, trying to hold onto his arms. He brings his feet down hard on their insteps, then pulls away fast.

                           JOHN
              April, run!

April hits the floor and grabs her gun. She comes up firing.

SWAT 1 gets a bullet in the face. Dies instantly. The patch flies from his hand.

SWAT 4 kicks April's gun out of her hand. She drops as he slashes at her with a short sword. It misses her by a hair.

Kanzaki draws a gun to shoot Chow in the confusion.

SWAT 4 intervenes, smokes Kanzaki before he can get off a shot.

April has her gun again. She fires. SWAT 4 gets it in the back of the head. He goes down.

> APRIL
>
> Drop it!

SWAT 2 and 3 ignore her and take evasive action. Chow heads for the door.

> JOHN
>
> April! Get out of here!

John battles the two surviving SWAT men. But they're better than him. He's getting pummeled and is barely holding his own.

> APRIL (O.S.)
>
> HEY!

The two SWAT men stop fighting John and turn to see April with a gun to Chow's head.

> APRIL (cont'd)
>
> Back off. Now!

The SWAT men hesitate.

> CHOW
>
> It's OK. Do what she says.

The SWAT men move away from John.

John goes to SWAT 1's corpse and removes a Devastator patch from his neck. Holds it up for April to see.

> JOHN
>
> Evidence.

April looks at the SWAT men, hard.

>   APRIL
>   Don't follow us.

John and April back away through the blown double-doors, with Chow. Making sure they don't trip over any dead bodies.

April keeps the gun to Chow's head. He's being cool about it.

>   CHOW
>   This is tedious, you know. Give up now and they
>   won't torture you. They'll make it clean.

John smacks Chow upside the head with his backhand.

>   JOHN
>   Are you excited now?

They make their way down the hall as fast as they can. The SWAT men don't follow.

>   APRIL
>   I don't like this.

John sees something attached to a wall nearby. Some kind of plastics bomb with a red light blinking on the detonator.

>   JOHN
>   Explosives!

He looks at Chow.

>   JOHN (cont'd)
>   These yours?

CHOW

I had my men kill anyone left alive and rig the place
for a final blowout. It'll all be blamed on you.

April lets Chow go so she can face him. She keeps her gun on
him. He steps back from her, cool and casual. Smile of a wolf.

APRIL

How do they go off?

Chow dropping from his sleeve like a hidden card, a small
pen-like device drops into his hand. He pups his thumb on the
button at one end.

CHOW

By remote.

APRIL

Drop it!

Chow almost presses the button. Looks at her hard.

CHOW

I drop it, it sets off the bombs. And I'm not handing it
over. In fact, either you let me walk or we all die.

APRIL

You won't kill yourself.

Chow makes like he's going to press it.

CHOW

Anything would be better than this conversation.

JOHN (to April)

We're both witnesses. We have evidence. They can
catch him later.

                         APRIL
    If they'll bother. Maybe I should just shoot him now.
    Save us the grief.

Chow holds up the device.

                         CHOW
    Maybe I should kill us all. Spare me from this ennui.

April gives Chow an angry jerk of her head telling him to
leave. He smiles and backs away, then disappears into a side
doorway.

John and April turn to run. But the house is a maze. Dead
bodies here and there.

                         APRIL
    Which way?

                         JOHN
              (shrugs)
    Left.

They enter a left hand door into a

INT. LIVING ROOM
The lights go out.

SWAT 2 leaps into the room, throwing a knife. April's gun
fires and leaves her hand. She's been cut.

John launches himself at the SWAT killer. They fight hard.

Blinking red lights in the dark tell April they have little time.
April grabs a chair, takes a swing at John's opponent.

The SWAT man spins, kicks. The chair explodes into pieces.

But the distraction was all John needs. Two harsh blows and the SWAT man is dead.

John grabs April's arm.

> JOHN
>> Come on!

They race for an exit and come out into

EXT. VAST ORIENTAL GARDEN
In the center, stands a large metal statue of a Japanese Samurai with a spear in one hand, looking fierce.

Dead guards lie in pools of blood. Dead attack dogs by their sides. One dead dog has its teeth around the neck of a SWAT corpse. There are a couple guns on the ground. April picks up a machine gun.

They look around. At the far end of the garden, Chow races into a large outbuilding with his assistant in tow.

> JOHN
>> Oh, shit...

Between them, SIX SWAT men appear, including the last survivor from the boardroom, SWAT 3. He's leading the pack.

They see April and John, and race toward them. Grinning.

April fires. They leap for cover drawing guns. One goes down. They fire back.

April and John take cover behind the statue.

Bullets chew up their hiding place. April's gun quickly runs out of ammo. There's nothing close by she can use.

                    APRIL
        We're done!

                    JOHN
        Maybe not.

John produces the patch he took as evidence from the dead SWAT man and starts to put it on his neck.

                    APRIL
        John, no! That'll kill you!

                    JOHN
        There should be time left on it.

He puts it on. His eyes go wide. Then narrows.

POV - JOHN
The world turns red. PULSING RED. Then turns hyper-real. Information is everywhere. Bullet trajectories and velocities as they fly by. He looks up and his enemies are forms, broken down as data.

John leaps out from his cover, a dynamo. The SWAT men stop shooting. They come at him with a vengeance.

The patch has added its own abilities to the previous patch's powers. Now John is amped WAY up!

BAM! He goes ballistic, like a dervish from Hell, he launches into them. It's an insane free-for-all.

April drops her empty gun, grabs another from a dead guard and races after Chow, who's already inside the outbuilding.

She takes shots at John's assailants as she runs. Two go down. The gun jams.

A killer races after her, leaving two for John. Knowing she's outclassed, April follows John's lead.

She pops out a PATCH from a dead SWAT man, removes her own and slaps on the Devastator patch just as SWAT 3 fires at her.

Her eyes flash for a second, as if she sees the world for the first time. Then she's moving.

April rolls, bullets ricochet where she was just a split second ago. She grabs a rock, throws it perfectly. SWAT 3's gun goes flying.

April's up. They go at it.

John and the two SWAT men battle fiercely.

April moves like a cat, leaping about to avoid her own foe.

The battle rages. John and April prevail.

April removes her patch quickly, picks up another gun. It's out of ammo.

                    APRIL
        Take out your patch before it fries you!

John smiles. He feels super-powerful and he doesn't want it to end.

                    JOHN
        But...

APRIL
Take it out!

A large noise from behind. They turn and see–

–The roof of the outbuilding opens wide. The sound of a helicopter can be heard.

JOHN
He's not getting away.

John races to the statue and steals the spear.

He LEAPS with the spear in one hand, CLIMBS and SCRAMBLES onto the roof of the house, as the copter begins to rise from the outbuilding.

APRIL
John, take it off! It'll kill you!

John ignores her. He races across the roof toward the outbuilding. The height advantage gives him one good shot at the copter.

INT. COPTER
Chow sees John, and plays his hand. Holding up the remote detonator.

CHOW
I told him he was going to lose, but would he listen? No. They never listen.

He pushes the button.

EXT. ROOFTOP
The house starts exploding in waves of intense fireballs.

John races across the roof as it goes up behind him, one blast after the other. He reaches the end of the roof as the whole thing seems to go up under him.

He simultaneously leaps like a madman, a blazing comet, propelled by the explosion, his clothes afire.

He THROWS the spear at the retreating copter and–

–It misses–

–But hits a revolving video billboard in the background, displaying commercials for Happy Patches.

The spear slams into the motor box that makes the sign revolve. SPARKS spritz from it and the BILLBOARD spins out of control.

It slams into the copter. Blades snap.

The copter crashes to the ground.

Chow is bloody, one arm broken. He tries to escape. His assistant, dead.

There's a loud metallic groan. Chow looks up in horror.

The billboard COLLAPSES onto the copter, crushing it in a blaze of shooting fireworks. The copter fuel ignites. KABOOM! Instant inferno.

John drops into a koi pond, burning. He convulses in the water, fires sizzling out. Then lies still.

His fires are extinguished and maybe his life, too.

APRIL

John!

April leaps in the pond, rushes to his side. She removes the patch from his neck. Tosses it.

She shakes him. Tears well up in her eyes.

APRIL (cont'd)
Don't die, damn you! Please!

Suddenly, he coughs and starts to come around.

APRIL (cont'd)
You OK?

JOHN
I've had better days.

APRIL
You've had worse?

John chuckles.

JOHN
No. And I hope I never do.

APRIL
That makes two of us.

They smile at each other, hug. Then get up to leave. The complex is blazing away. Sirens are getting louder.

APRIL (cont'd)
My boss said I should type up a resume. I agree.
There's got to be a better place than this.

                    JOHN
         I hear Seattle's nice.

                    APRIL
         Except for the rain.

They laugh.

John and April head off into the night, arm and arm, as the video billboards continue their relentless hustle.

                              FADE OUT.

                   THE END

ABOUT THE AUTHOR

James D. HUDNALL has been writing professionally since 1986. He is best known for his comic book series *ESPers*, *The Psycho*, *Harsh Realm* (which was made into a Fox TV series, now on DVD), *Lex Luthor: The Unauthorized Biography*, *Sinking, Streets* and *The Age of Heroes*. His current work includes *2 to the Chest* and *Aftermath* for French publisher Les Humanoïdes. Hudnall lives in Las Vegas, Nevada, likes to travel and is furiously working on more screenplays. For more information, his website is: http://jameshudnall.com.